TOUCHDOWNS
&
TEMPTATIONS

Our books are also available in paperback.
Find our catalog on:
https://cherry-publishing.com/en/

MRS KRISTAL

TOUCHDOWNS
&
TEMPTATIONS

Cherry Publishing

ISBN: 978-1-80116-820-5

1

CARA

I grab my purse and take one last look in the mirror before I head downstairs. I am going to meet my best friend Marina for a drink in the city and I can't wait!

I've been back in my hometown of Boston for a week. I haven't found an apartment to rent yet, so I'm staying with my parents for now, but it's just temporary, I really need my own place.

I graduated from the University of California. My dad was coaching the Oakland Pirates at the time, so it was a good fit for me. We had already lived on the West Coast for a few years.

My dad is none other than former Boston Foxes quarterback: Michael Corse. He is a legend here. I spent most of my childhood in Boston, which is why I call it my hometown. Of course, my dad's job took us to other cities in the US, but Boston was always our home.

I put my hand on the dark gray banister of the grand staircase in the foyer and walk down. Personally, I find the villa too ostentatious, but my parents like it as a retirement home.

My new job in my dad's company, Corse Sports Management, starts next week. I know I can always count on my parents for support, but it's time for me to stand on my own two feet. Which is ridiculous coming from me, since I'm going to inherit fifty million dollars and own one of the biggest sports management agencies in the US.

As the child of a sports star, I was in the spotlight from an early age. The public always wanted to be a part of my life, growing up, I don't know why. I haven't done anything interesting enough to write articles about. I'm just Michael Corse's daughter. My entire childhood consisted of cheering for my dad in front of the TV or in a VIP box at the stadium. He's a great dad, but damn, he is, first and foremost, a sports superstar to most Americans and will always be a National Football League legend.

It's hard to imagine what my life would be like if I had been a boy.

"Hello," I greet my parents as I walk into the dining room. They are sitting together at a table that is way too big, with sushi spread out in front of them.

"Hi Honey," my mom says smiling at me. "Do you have a date?"

"I'm meeting Marina," I reply, stealing a sushi roll and shoving it into my mouth.

"You want a plate with that?" my dad jokes, giving me a warm smile. He's really enjoyed spending time with us over the last few years, and still does. He is totally against me moving out. He keeps saying that the house is big enough for me to have my own space, but I want to be completely independent. I mean, as much as I can be while working for them.

"I have to go," I say, shoving another sushi roll into my mouth, "I'll just have one more."

"Cara!" Mom gives me a dirty look. "That's not ladylike. I've raised you better than that."

"I don't really care, Mom," I lick my fingertips. "I'm out of here. Love you guys."

"Love you too, sweetheart," she calls after me, and I hurry

through the foyer to leave the villa.

My red Ferrari is parked out front, glistening in the sun. I pull the key from my purse and unlock the door. The headlights come on and I open the driver's door to get in. I don't really care about my parents' wealth. My best friend Marina comes from an ordinary family, and my parents were born into the working class. But if I'm going to spend millions of dollars on something, it's going to be a car. There's nothing like an awesome car to cruise the streets of Boston in. I own five of them now. That may be a bit much, but damn - I love cars. Especially when they sparkle and shine as beautifully as my Ferrari or let me sit as high and elegantly as my Range Rover. When I want to take it easy, I take my Mini. It's the most low-key car I own.

The Ferrari's engine roars, I put it in reverse and leave the driveway.

★★★

The bar where I'm meeting Marina is in downtown Boston. I pull into a parking space and turn off the engine. I take my sunglasses and a baseball cap out of my purse. It's probably overkill, but I hate being photographed.

After one last look in the mirror, I get out of the car. I'm sure people wonder how a young woman like me can afford a car like that. They probably ask themselves: 'Who paid for it? Her father? Her husband / boyfriend? Or maybe her sugar daddy?'

I mean, it's not exactly a lie, my dad did pay for it. But in the age of social media and influencers, I can get money on my own. The only problem is that I don't like being out in public.

I lock the car and enter the bar. Marina is sitting at a table and waves as soon as she sees me.

Touchdowns &Temptations

I walk over to her, and she stands up to greet me. "Hi," I say, giving her a kiss on the cheek. "How are you?"

"Fine and you?" she asks.

I put my bag down and sit across from her. "Me too," I reply. "Have you ordered yet?"

"I was waiting for you."

I open the menu and study it carefully. I decide on a coffee and a water. After putting the menu back in the holder, I immediately look at Marina.

"So, tell me," I ask her. "How's Caleb? How's the move going?"

Caleb is Marina's fiancé and a complete jerk, in my opinion, but my best friend loves him. He's a lawyer, and they met at a Boston Foxes game when Marina was my +1. As soon as he opened his mouth, I knew he wasn't going to make her happy. However, two years have passed, and he has put a ring on her finger. My hopes that she would find someone who was really right for her are pretty much shattered.

"Well," my best friend says, "it's not going fast enough."

I raise my eyebrows and look at her questioningly. I wasn't expecting such a cryptic answer. Especially since she's grinning at me like something's up. Without a word, Marina pushes a photo across the table. Surprised, I grab it. My best friend grins even wider and when I pick it up, my breath catches in my throat. It's an ultrasound with her name on it and the caption: 'Will you be my godmother?'

I scream happily, causing the guests at the next table to look over at us. But I don't care.

"Oh my God!" Still completely stunned, I slap my hand over my mouth. "You... you're pregnant."

"Yes." She sniffles and tears come to her eyes. "I wanted to tell you in person. The baby is due in mid-February."

My best friend is going to have her first baby. Wow! It's unbelievable and I'm so happy for Marina. She's always wanted to be a mother at a young age. And even though I don't particularly like Caleb, she has everything it takes to start a family. Marina is a year older than me, and Caleb is twenty-six. They're the perfect age to start a family. He also comes from an influential family in Boston and can offer her a good life.

"You're having a baby. I can't believe it. And we can't even celebrate properly," I grumble.

Marina giggles. "You wouldn't believe how hard it was to keep this a secret. Caleb and I have been to so many receptions and weddings this summer," she says.

I've never met anyone who acts so serious but has such little impact on society like Caleb does. No matter how well off his family is. They're not a part of the upper class of Boston, and secretly, of course, he knows that. Caleb is an arrogant guy and tells everyone, and I mean *everyone*, that his future wife is the best friend of Cara Corse, the daughter of Boston Foxes' legend Michael Corse. Whether the person wants to know it or not. If I didn't know better, I'd say he'd rather fuck me than Marina.

I shake off my thoughts about this idiot and ask Marina all kinds of questions about her pregnancy. I want to know everything. When and how she found out, how she told Caleb and how he reacted. I also ask about the reaction of her parents and her future in-laws.

"Don't turn around," she says out of the blue and looks at me mysteriously. Of course I want to turn around. Marina grabs my hand to get my attention. "Cara, I'm serious, don't."

"Why?" I ask impatiently.

"There are two guys at the bar," she explains. "One has dark hair, and the other is blond. And I think the blond one is interested in you. He keeps looking over. They look familiar..."

Now I *really* want to turn around and see.

"Are you sure?" I ask Marina and she nods.

"From the look of it, the dark-haired guy is trying to convince the other one to come and talk to you."

"And why wouldn't he be interested in you and not me, uh?" I ask, sipping at my water. My throat is suddenly dry. Marina is a beautiful woman. Her long blonde hair, her full lips and her constant good mood attract a lot of men. "It's not necessarily obvious that you're pregnant and engaged."

Marina rolls her eyes and points to her overly flashy engagement ring. Okay ... this bling is actually visible from several miles away. She loves it but I think it's a bit much. It's like Caleb has to constantly brag about how much money he has. Which isn't actually his since he's an heir, just like me.

"I think my ring says it all," she says, looking at it for a few seconds. "I'm telling you; the blonde guy is into you."

"You're probably imagining it," I chuckle. "But, okay. Let's say he wants me..." I can't believe I'm going along with this. "That doesn't mean I want him too, does it?"

"Why?" asks Marina. "Don't be so uptight all the time, Cara. I'm not saying you should marry him. I'm talking about sex. Amazing sex."

"I'm not uptight," I contradict her immediately. "I'm just not into that sort of thing. I never have been."

"I know," she reassures me. "But I think he really would be worth an exception. Oh my God, he's getting up."

Marina is making it sound like it's a rom-com, and we're the love interests. She screams almost as loudly as I did when I saw the ultrasound. While it was an appropriate reaction for me, her hormones seem to have taken over. She is completely crazy.

"Maybe he needs to go to the bathroom?" I think.

"No," Marina says. "The bathroom is on the other way."

I don't feel like talking about the guy anymore, so I push

the thoughts about him out of my head.

"Let's forget about the guy and talk about my first day at Corse Sports Management, okay?" I ask my best friend.

"He's coming over,"" she says, completely ignoring my suggestion. My heart skips a beat, and I bite my lip nervously.

"Marina?" I ask. "Can we talk about my job?"

"We're not going to talk about your job when you have the opportunity to have the best sex of your life," she hisses at me. "Get it?"

"You're crazy!" I roll my eyes and Marina giggles.

"He's coming," she informs me. "Come on, throw your napkin down."

"I am not doing that. Pregnancy is making you crazy."

"Come on!" she urges. "He'll be here any minute."

My God, this is unbelievable.

"Marina, no!" I protest. "You can forget it."

"Do it!"

I ignore her and reach for my fork to eat my shrimp when she deliberately kicks me in the shin. I almost scream in pain and drop my fork.

"Tell me, are you nuts?" I look at her angrily and am about to reach for the fork to end this embarrassing situation when someone else grabs it. A hand that wasn't there before, a man's hand. Our hands touch and I jump back, startled. An electric shock runs through my body and when I look up, I see the most beautiful blue eyes I have ever seen.

I swallow hard as his intense gaze knocks my socks off, and I let go of the fork. Suddenly I straighten up and he does the same. As he stands in front of me, I can't help but form my lips into a silent 'Wow'.

He has broad shoulders that you want to lean on, perfect muscles, and arms so strong that they make you want to 'accidentally' let yourself fall into. My eyes move up to his face, and he grins at me. His lips are thin, and his cheeks are adorned with a blond shadow of a beard, which matches his short hair.

"You dropped this," he says, handing me the fork. Heat rises in my cheeks in record time, and I can't catch my breath.

"Thank you," I reply, feeling ashamed, and I give my best friend a bitter look. I've made a complete fool of myself in front of this Adonis[1]. "I'm sorry, I'm clumsy." My apology doesn't make it any better, and when the corners of his mouth lift, I notice that he's amused.

"That's okay," he says. "But you should probably ask for a new fork."

"Yes, I'll do that."

I suck at flirting. I've never been the kind of girl who can get a guy to fall for her with just a few glances. Unlike my best friend, I'm shy and always worried about saying the wrong thing. It's really starting to take its toll now.

"I'm Noah," he introduces himself and shakes my hand. "And who do I have the pleasure of meeting?"

"Cara," I whisper. "My name is Cara."

"Right then, Cara," he says. "See you around, and don't forget the new fork."

He winks at me, making my face look like a tomato within seconds, and then heads for the door marked 'Restroom'.

I slap my forehead with my free hand and look at Marina. "Oh my God," I mutter. "Well... that was awkward."

"Yes, it was," she confirms. "It was like a car crash. I just couldn't look away. It was awful."

---

1 *In Greek Mythology, Adonis was the lover of Aphrodite and Persephone. He was considered to be the ideal of male beauty.*

2

NOAH

I can't believe that I acted so stupidly when I approached Cara. As soon as she entered the bar, all I could see was her. Her slender legs, the short dress, the shoulder-length black hair, and the friendly smile that took over the room. My god, I was immediately smitten. Alex annoyed me for almost half an hour, trying to convince me to approach her and ask her out for a drink.

My twin brother kept bugging me until I got up and went over to her. When I was almost at her table, she dropped her fork, and I took the opportunity to talk to her. When I saw her face, with her dark brown eyes looking right at me, I was speechless. And because I couldn't think of anything better to say than my name, I told her to get a new fork. It couldn't have been more awkward. Her friend didn't take her eyes off us and told her for sure that I was the biggest idiot ever.

Sighing, I look in the mirror in front of me and rest my hands on the top of the sink. Even though this attempt at flirting backfired, I don't have to hide. I look good, I'm in my prime at twenty-five, and I have the best damn job in the world. Why on earth shouldn't I be able to meet a woman like that?

In most cases, all I have to do is tell women that I'm Noah

McCarter and it becomes a no-brainer. Being the quarterback of the Boston Foxes basically gives you a free pass.

After washing and drying my hands, I stand to my full height. To boost my battered ego, I flex my muscles and grin smugly.

I'm a cool guy. I can walk up to a woman I like, ask her out, and lure her into my bed! And now I want Cara in my bed.

"You can do it, McCarter," I encourage myself. "She's an ordinary woman."

I turn and confidently leave the bathroom to talk to Cara again. I notice with regret that the table where she was with her friend is empty.

I glance through the bar and out onto the street to see if I can spot her, but nothing. She's gone.

"Damn!" Annoyed, I cross the bar and sit down with my brother. Alex looks at me sympathetically. Since he dyed his hair brown, we don't look much alike. But if you look closely, you can't deny that we are identical twins, despite our different hair colors. Alex is two minutes older than me, which he never fails to point out. We grew up with our big brother Logan in a small town outside of Nashville. Logan plays tight end for the Nashville Warriors. We started playing American football in high school and had athletic scholarships in college. Alex went to Utah, and I went to Georgia. We got drafted three years ago. Alex was drafted by the Boston Foxes, and I was drafted by the Miami Sharks until I followed him to Boston this year.

"What was that?" asks Alex, raising his eyebrows.

"Nothing," I grumble, dropping onto the barstool. "In fact, nothing at all."

I reach for my beer and take a big gulp.

"Yeah, I can see that," Alex replies, not very gallantly. "What happened? You didn't even get her number. Since when do you suck at flirting?"

I roll my eyes and take another sip of my beer before answering. "She dropped her fork, and I picked it up," I summarize the situation he saw for himself. "I introduced myself, she introduced herself, and then I told her to get a new fork because hers was dirty."

Alex tries to remain serious but fails miserably. The next moment he bursts out laughing, causing the bartender to give us a quizzical look.

"Oh God, Noah." Alex is clearly enjoying himself. "I thought you were going to buy her a drink and ask for her number."

"I know," I hiss. "When did she leave?"

"Shortly after you disappeared into the bathroom, they called the waitress and paid," he replies. "You must have scared her off." I roll my eyes. "But wait..." I look at him intently. Ever since we were little boys, he's been such a drama queen, always procrastinating. "Since I had nothing better to do, I followed them, and your sweetie got into a Ferrari."

I open my eyes and turn my head toward the door to look out at the street. "A Ferrari?" I ask. "Are you sure?"

"Yep, I can recognize a baby like that," he replies. "Great ride. She definitely has taste and a great benefactor."

I frown.

"Benefactor? What does that mean?"

"How old do you think she is?" he says, pretending to really think. "Early or mid-twenties at the most. A woman that age can't afford a two-hundred-thousand-dollar Ferrari."

"Why not?" I ask, "Maybe she has a business."

What is so surprising about the fact that a woman can make a lot of money at a young age? Take Miley Cyrus or the Olsen twins. They were multimillionaires as teenagers.

"Or a rich boyfriend, or no, wait ..." The drama queen is back. "A sugar daddy? Rich parents?"

Now his imagination takes over.

"She doesn't have a sugar daddy!" I grimace and shake my head vehemently. I don't want to believe that she has a sugar daddy. How disgusting would that be? Such a beautiful woman, with such a beautiful body, and then she lets some old dude fuck her to drive a Ferrari? "No way!"

"You just don't want to admit it," Alex teases, winking at me. "And if she doesn't, she has very rich parents."

"And what's wrong with that?" I want to know.

"Well." Alex shrugs. "You're a little boy from Tennessee who knows how to throw a ball."

I can't help but laugh and look at my brother.

"And what are you?" I ask immediately. "A little boy from Tennessee who's good at catching balls?" He grins and nods. "So... what's wrong with that?"

"Get her out of your mind," he advises me. "She's probably going to marry someone from a rich family or have an up-and-coming politician at her side. But not a professional athlete from Tennessee. You know what Mom always says."

I sigh. Our mother is very worried and afraid that we will never find a good wife but will spend our lives being courted by TV starlets and models. She is very old-fashioned and would prefer that we marry a woman from the neighborhood, or at least from the same county.

"That the best girls and later wives are on a farm in Tennessee?" Alex nods. "I still want her," I decide. "Mom will get used to the fact that we'll never marry these girls."

"And how are you going to do that?" Alex looks at me with interest. "You only know her first name and you know her car. Well ... I know her car because it was gone when you came back. That's not much."

Damn, it really isn't much, but I'm not giving up hope.

"Maybe she'll come back soon," I think aloud. "Then I'll

talk to her again." Alex looks far from convinced, but he nods.

"You don't like the idea?"

"No." He shakes his head. "Boston is huge, if you count the metropolitan area and the state of Massachusetts, even bigger. How do you plan on seeing her again?"

"Hope dies last," I make a vague prediction.

"It died when she left the bar, dude," Alex replies.

I sigh and grab my beer. I wish I had just opened my mouth.

A Few Days Later

I park my Bentley in front of Corse Sports Management headquarters and turn off the engine. I fired my agent a few weeks ago and am looking for a new one. The collaboration was no longer satisfactory, and the contracts he was negotiating were ridiculous. Certainly not at the level of an elite quarterback. Some of my colleagues are being handled by the agency owned by our former quarterback and club legend Michael Corse. I made an appointment with him to possibly do business together. Without exception, the guys are happy and say that Corse knows exactly what's important because of his own experience as a pro. He knows the details of the contracts, which clauses not to sign and which collaborations to accept and which not to. I've had that experience over the years, but it's always nice to be represented by someone who knows the players' situation. So far, everything they've offered me has sounded promising.

I have my appointment with Mrs. Corse. I know Corse has a daughter my age, but I can't remember what she looks like, I haven't seen a photo of her in a while. The last one was taken a few years ago at Corse's official induction into the Boston

Foxes Hall of Fame. Cara Catherine Corse is her name. It's almost ironic that she has the same first name as the pretty brunette from the bar a few days ago. I still can't get her out of my mind and I'm thinking about how I can see her again. Alex thinks my thoughts are ridiculous and doesn't support my plans at all. You'd think my twin was making fun of me.

The Bentley's lights flash as I lock up and head for the main entrance of Corse Sports Management. The entrance hall has a black marble floor, a seating area with black furniture, and the reception desk, where a woman my mother's age sits, is also black with silver highlights and the company logo branded into the counter.

I walk over and smile at her.

"Good morning. Noah McCarter," I introduce myself. "I have an appointment with Ms. Corse."

"Good morning," she replies friendly. "Ms. Corse is expecting you. Please follow me."

I nod as she stands and circles the reception desk. When she looks at me, she has to tilt her head back.

"Thank you," I say, letting her lead me through the large lobby to the elevator. As you would expect, it is glassed in and offers a wonderful view of the company as you go up and down.

"Ms. Corse's office is on the third floor next to her father's."

I nod.

To be honest, I want an experienced agent who has been in the business for years and can get me the best deals. Not a young woman who got the job through daddy's favor. As his daughter, I doubt that she had to interview for the job, or even show a résumé and references to secure the job.

"How old is Ms. Corse?" I ask, and the woman looks at me in surprise.

"Sorry?" she asks nicely, offering me a way out.

"Forget it," I mumble. "It's not that important."

And really, it's none of my business how old Ms. Corse is.

"No, no," the woman continues. "I just didn't hear you right." She smiles at me and taps the little hearing aid in her left ear. "Please repeat the question."

So much for her giving me an out.

"I asked how old Ms. Corse is," I repeat.

"She is twenty-two years old," she replies, eyeing me suspiciously. "Is that a problem?"

Fortunately, before I can answer, the elevator stops, and we get out. I don't know if that's a problem. Twenty-two is extremely young. To me, that means she just graduated from college. We all know that she only has this job because Corse is her father. Under other circumstances, she probably wouldn't even be allowed to make coffee for clients like me. My next problem is that if I really like Corse Sports Management, I can't criticize the owner's daughter. Right?

"Please wait here," she asks me.

I nod and agree. I take my phone out of my pocket.

+1 new message from Alex

Alex: *How is it going?*
Noah: *I just got into the office.*

"Mr. McCarter is here now, Ms. Corse." The employee doesn't speak very quietly. "Shall I invite him in?"

I can't hear Ms. Corse's answer, no matter how hard I try. But when the woman turns to me, whose name I either still don't know or haven't memorized, I know I can enter.

"Please," she says, making an inviting gesture with her hand. I nod and walk past her into the office.

"Thank you," I say as my last word to her.

And as soon as I enter Ms. Corse's office, I am stunned.

Standing in front of me is the woman from the bar I was trying to get out of my mind.

This can't be true. I can't be that lucky, can I?

Cara. My Cara from the bar is Cara Catherine Corse? Holy shit.

I stare at her with my mouth hanging open, and she seems to still be getting over the initial shock of seeing me like this.

"Mr. McCarter," she greets me in a businesslike tone that irritates me at first. I picked up her fork. Wow, that sounds even dumber than 'I carried a watermelon' from *Dirty Dancing*[2].

Cara comes over and holds out her hand.

I look at her without saying a word. Cara is wearing a knee-length, tight-fitting red dress with long sleeves and a round neckline that looks nice and seems perfectly appropriate for the office. The high heels on her feet make her look much taller than she is. Her makeup is heavier than in the bar. Her lips are a seductive red and her hair is loose over her shoulders.

"Nice to meet you. Cara Corse. Welcome to Corse Sports Management."

She extends her hand invitingly, which I take.

"Hello," I reply a little grumpy because she doesn't greet me more personally. "Noah McCarter. Nice to meet you too."

---

2 *Dirty Dancing* is an American romantic drama dance film (1987).

3

CARA

Seeing Noah again as my new client is a shock. Our meeting at the bar was not only too short, but also incredibly awkward. I had hoped he would come back so we could talk some more. But Marina suddenly felt sick. An unpleasant side effect of pregnancy. So, she asked me to drive her home.

I've been thinking about Noah for the past few days. Now he's standing in my office and wants me to represent him from now on. At least that's what I think. I never expected him to be a professional athlete, let alone the quarterback of the Boston Foxes. I have to say that I'm not particularly interested in football. The players are just people like you and me. Not demi-gods, as many fans like to claim. Their private lives interest me even less. Noah is supposed to get the Foxes back on track this season and take over from my dad. I've heard his name a few times because my dad has nothing else to talk about at the moment. I wish I had listened to him more and googled the new quarterback. Then I would have known that Noah from the bar and Noah McCarter, quarterback of the Boston Foxes, are one and the same.

"Why don't you take a seat," I offer him timidly. "What can I get you to drink?"

Noah looks at me skeptically but says nothing as he sits

down on the couch in my office. I take the documents and my MacBook off the desk and sit down in the chair next to him. Admittedly, he looks even better than he did a few days ago in the bar. The shadow of his beard is more pronounced, and his black shirt clings to his toned chest. The top buttons are undone, giving me a glimpse of his tanned skin. This man is incredibly sexy and handsome.

But he's still a quarterback, so he is off-limits to me. I don't want to organize my life around sports and their schedules, as my mother has done for almost thirty years.

"Nothing, thanks," he says, smiling at me. Noah rests his forearms on his thighs. I notice he has a tattoo on his left wrist. An L and an A with a crown, I must admit that I really like it. I know he has at least one brother, named Alexander or as everyone calls him: Alex. He's a running back for the Boston Foxes. Of course, I know that from my dad because he's always raving about how the brothers play together.

"First of all, I'd like to talk to you about what you expect from us, and then I'll tell you ...", but as I begin to talk, I notice that he isn't listening to me. "Is everything okay?"

"Honestly, no." He clears his throat and rubs his hands together. "Don't take this the wrong way, Ms. Corse, but I wasn't expecting you. Are you just having this first conversation to get to know me, or are you planning on representing me in the future?"

I look at him a little surprised. I hadn't expected this. Of course, I'm supposed to represent him in the future. He's going to be my first big client, and I'm very proud of that. My dad wouldn't put that much trust in me, and possibly even jeopardize the company's good reputation if he didn't have absolute confidence in my abilities.

"I don't understand," I whisper, lowering my pen. "Could you please be more precise?"

"Of course!" Noah looks at me firmly. "Corse Sports Management was recommended to me by my colleagues who have been consulting here for years." I nod, but I know he's not finished. "I made this appointment to get a first impression. Now I'm asking you if this is an introductory meeting or if you're my new agent."

"Would that be bad?" I blurt out rather unprofessionally.

"Yes!"

It's like a slap in the face for me, and I'm completely flustered. Heat rises in my cheeks, and I feel uncomfortable because he doesn't want to work with me. I've been preparing for this interview all morning because I want to prove to my father and myself that I'm in the right place, not because I'm going to own this company one day. I'm good at my job, and Noah McCarter is my ticket to the world of sports management. I thought because we're the same age, we'd be similar, and we'd have a great working relationship for years to come. But now he's taking the wind out of my sails.

"Oh, okay," I whisper. "May I know why?"

"You're too young," he replies bluntly. "I need an experienced agent who knows the business and knows exactly what I need and what sums he has to negotiate for me. I don't think you..."

"I can do it!" I blurt out.

His eyebrows rise skeptically. I feel unfairly treated by him and want a chance. "I mean, I know what I'm doing and what you expect of me."

"How many clients have you taken care of?" he wants to know.

"I think that's..." I try to evade his question.

"Give me a number," he demands and his gaze penetrates me. This has nothing to do with the friendly man in the bar who flirted with me. Sitting in front of me is a tough businessman and athlete who wants to be well represented.

Fuck.

Why didn't my dad warn me? He knows what some of these guys are like, and yet he let me have this conversation. On the other hand, I shouldn't have talked so big. I was bragging about how I was going to outplay that quarterback. I don't give a shit, and now I'm embarrassing myself in front of him, again. Then later I will do the same with my dad, who will tell me he knew.

"I have ... well ... I am ..." I stammer to myself.

"So, none," he concludes and stands up. I watch him as calmly as possible. When he stands in front of me at full height, I am overwhelmed by his presence. I didn't feel that way in the bar.

"I'm sorry, but that's not possible. I'm not going to be a guinea pig for the boss's daughter."

Now I stand up and stare at him angrily. That was definitely too much. Even though he still towers over me by at least twenty centimeters. It's not fair to insinuate that I only have this job because my father owns the company.

"I went to the University of California for four years, I interned with the Oakland Pirates, and I know this fucking business better than you think. Don't tell me you're a guinea pig for my career because you think I'm 'daddy's girl'. I continue. "I'm going to own this company one day. Do you really think I want to put Corse Sports Management or myself in a bad light?"

Noah opens his mouth and closes it.

"I'm good!" I make it clear again and look at him hard. "Give me a chance - please." My tone softens at the end, and I point to the couch. "Sit down." He hesitates, but when I sit down, he follows me.

"I'm sorry," I mumble. "I shouldn't have freaked out like

I did, but I know what I'm doing. Why don't you let me explain?"

"Go ahead, explain," he repeats, his mouth twisting. "I fired my old agent because he explained too much and did too little. He negotiated bad deals, and that's why my salary is what it is. I can't imagine the daughter of Foxes legend Michael Corse negotiating a better salary for me."

His blue eyes flash aggressively at me.

"Oh yeah?" I grin at him mischievously. "Why don't you let me try?"

"Try," he mumbles, shaking his head. "I wouldn't want to embarrass myself in front of the new bosses."

"Then keep your measly salary of ..." I open the documents. When I see the number next to his annual salary, I gasp. "Ten million dollars?"

"I wanted at least twelve million," he counters.

"Of course," I scoff, managing not to roll my eyes. "Noah, that's insane. Your contract is for five years, you get millions in bonuses, and you're the only player who gets an extra bonus if you win the Super Bowl. Which, as you know, you haven't won yet. You can't ask for more than that."

"Why not?" he counters.

I seriously wonder which one of us is the supposed professional.

"Because it's too bold," I reply bluntly. "Do you know what the employees make? Maybe two thousand dollars a month. That's what your shoes cost." I point at his black oxfords. "Your salary is more than enough. Besides, you'll look greedy when we try to negotiate new contracts, and you'll fall out of favor with the fans and the bosses. Then they'll boo you and question you. What do you think the Foxes bosses will do to you?"

"Hm." Noah looks pensive and rubs his chin. "Maybe

you're not wrong."

"Really?" I ask, looking at him with wide eyes.

"Yes!" he replies, rubbing his huge hands over his face. "Maybe my salary is enough, but you have to understand that I'm skeptical. This collaboration is not what I want!"

He looks at me and his gaze goes right through me.

I don't understand his problem. I can do the job just as well as someone who has been in the business for thirty years. Maybe even better because I'm quicker to see the ravages of time. But Noah doesn't seem to see it that way.

"Why?" I ask sourly. "Because I'm not fifty, I don't have over thirty years of professional experience and I can't show you a list of my clients. Just so you know, I'm no worse than they are."

"I'm not saying you're worse," he replies tense. "You're young and inexperienced."

"And how am I supposed to gain experience if everyone I meet thinks like you?" I shake my head. "If you don't want to work with me, that's fine with me, but be honest about it."

Noah doesn't say anything again but stands up and runs his fingers through his hair. He paces up and down my office, which really annoys me. I'm not here to convince a spoiled quarterback to work with me. He has to want to, and if he doesn't, I'm afraid I can't help him. "Mr. McCarter," I correct myself. "It's not a problem for me, but we need to talk about it clearly now."

"And we're back to 'Mr. McCarter' now?" He grins at me, and I can't help but grin back. Noah is right. It's stupid of me to call him Mr. McCarter again.

"All right, Ms. Corse," he says with a grin. "I'm really interested in working with Corse Sports Management, but I remain skeptical."

I puff out my cheeks and tilt my head back.

"We're not going to get anywhere like this," I conclude.

"Go out with me," he says suddenly, and I start to laugh.

"What?"

"Go out with me," he asks again. "Tonight, you and me, dinner."

"Why?" I ask, my eyes following him. Noah smiles and licks his lips with his tongue.

God, that's sexy.

"Because that's what I wanted to ask you at the bar. If you'd go out with me and I'd get your number."

Now he has completely surprised me. This has nothing to do with a professional business meeting.

"Uh." I'm at a loss for words. "I can't do that because I don't have a private relationship with my clients."

"Then the decision is made," he says, shoving his hands into his pockets. "I want the date. Without it, there will be no collaboration."

"You're kidding?" I gasp and stand up.

"No."

"This is blackmail, Noah." I brush my hair back anxiously. "You want to pick a date that could go badly over working for Corse Sports Management? Did I get that right?"

This guy is crazy. This is stupid, I think he got hit on the head one too many times during practice.

"I'm convinced that our date won't go badly." He sounds confident. "And so, yes. I'd rather get to know you than working with this company."

"You're crazy!" I blurt out uncontrollably again. You want to be professional and land a big fish, but instead you just start talking. And all because he wants a date? "This is getting completely out of hand," I add much more thoughtfully.

"Why?" he asks.

"Why?" it shoots out of me again. "None of this was

planned. I wanted to prove to myself and my dad that I could do this. Instead, you ask me out on a date, and I freak out. Now please don't tell me that something hasn't gotten out of hand."

He doesn't react and just looks at me.

"You convinced me," he says, licking his lips as his eyes take a clearly ambiguous look at my body. The heat spreads through me again. I have to stay professional. No matter how hot I think he is.

"Noah!" I clench my hands and stare at him angrily. "I'm here as your new agent, not as dating material."

"I like you better as dating material," he purrs, and I roll my eyes.

"You're impossible."

"So, our date?" he insists, putting his hands on his hips. "And then we'll see about collaborating professionally?"

"Are you blackmailing me?" My eyebrows knit inquiringly as my fingernails dig painfully into my palms. I feel like I'm boiling.

"Maybe," he says, winking at me. "A little. We both get what we want. I get the date and you get your client. A classic win-win situation."

"No," I say, shaking my head. "I can't do that. It's unprofessional."

Noah takes a step toward me and sighs.

"Cara," he calls me by my first name for the first time and it sounds really nice. I look at him and, as expected, he is smiling. "Give yourself a break."

"No," I insist, causing him to roll his eyes. Noah walks over to my desk and leans against it. He crosses his arms over his chest.

"What's this about, Noah?" I want to know. "I'm here to work, not to flirt."

"Too bad," he replies. "I like flirting with you."

I groan inwardly. He's so childish. He's probably enjoying it right now.

"I can tell," I reply. "I want to represent you because I'm sure we'll make a good team. But we are not going on a date!"

"Come on!" Noah pushes himself off the desk and walks over to me. "It's a date, Cara. Just a dinner. What's going to happen?"

He can't be serious, can he? A lot can happen. Like me liking him even more than I already do. That could happen. Or he wants another date. He's already blackmailing me.

"No!" I insist, turning to pack my things and put them on my desk. "I'm not going out with you."

"Too bad," he says. "You can request my previous work from my former agent. Read it and call me when you have time."

Irritated that he changed the subject so abruptly, I look at him. I'm tempted to ask him if this is a trick, but I don't dare. The last thing I want is to upset him again.

"See you then." Noah nods at me again and heads for the office door.

"Oh, and Cara," he says suddenly, turning to me. "Please send me an e-mail to let me know when it's convenient for our date. After all, it's a give and take. See you then."

And then he's gone!

4

CARA

I can't get Noah's immoral offer to trade a job for a date out of my head. I know that I should decline. What will I do if he bails on me? He gets the date and then he's over the hill and gets another agent. He seemed very certain when he said he didn't want to work with me. In fact, he's not interested in working with me professionally at all. I can somewhat understand his skepticism. I'm twenty-two years old and I don't have the same professional experience as a thirty-year-old agent. I realize that, but he doesn't have the experience as a quarterback that my dad has, and yet the team and the club trust him. Young people need experience.

Maybe my comparison is a little flawed because my dad will never be able to do the physical things that Noah does today. Still, it wouldn't be fair to deny him a chance just because he's old.

No matter how I look at it, Noah won't work with me until I go out with him. That's a fucking problem.

What do I do if he keeps asking for more and more? One date for a job and another for a deal. God, I can spin this wheel over and over again. On the other hand, every date I go on secures another collaboration and my reputation as a consultant in the industry. It's not the worst business, but ... no. An agent doesn't date the first player she's assigned. Especially not the quarterback of the Boston Foxes.

My reputation in the business would be ruined. Going from 'daddy's girl' to 'NFL bitch' who gets it on with the superstar.

Great career, Cara!

I should stop thinking about the fact that I really like Noah and instead gather the facts and my own resolutions: Never date a professional athlete!

Don't end up like your mom!

My parents have been together for over twenty years, and my mom loves my dad very much, but I know too well how often she felt lonely when he had to travel across the country.

That's not the life I want to live as a grown woman, much less the life I want my children to live. What if Noah is traded by the Foxes in a year? Will we move then? Does he expect his girlfriend to follow him wherever he goes?

My mind is going completely crazy. I haven't even agreed to a date with the guy and I'm already thinking about not moving for him. Wow.

I turn off the engine of my Ferrari and get out of the car. On my way to the front door, I hope my father isn't home and doesn't want to know about the current state of the negotiations. He won't be happy that I couldn't win Noah over right away. More importantly, he won't be happy that I couldn't get him to sign with Corse Sports Management. He is my father, and he loves me, but, of course, he is also a businessman and I am his employee.

As soon as I enter the villa, I hear him calling: "Cara?"

I sigh.

"Is that you?" he adds.

"Yes," I reply, walking into the kitchen. He is standing at the kitchen island, stirring his espresso. He looks at me with a smile. "Hey Dad," I greet him.

"Hello," he says, and I can see in his eyes how eager he is to hear more about my meeting with Noah.

"How did it go with McCarter?" is his next question.

I bite my lower lip and consider for a second whether to tell him the truth. That it went rather badly, and that Noah is trying to blackmail me.

"Fine," I lie instead and put on a smile. "It went really well ... we ... we got ... we discussed our collaboration thoroughly."

I don't sound nearly as confident as I want to. My father raises his eyebrows and looks at me questioningly.

I sigh. "He was a little worried because I'm only twenty-two."

"I didn't expect that from him. He doesn't seem like that at all," he replies thoughtfully.

"Hm," I mutter.

I raise my arms and shrug.

"But don't worry, Daddy," I say, more to myself than to him. "I'll get him under contract. Just give me two more days."

"Why two?"

"Why not?" I ask the counter question. "I'll send him another e-mail and get all the information from his last agent You'll see - I can do it!"

"You will," he replies, smiling at me. "You're my daughter after all." He winks at me. I smile weakly, but my father is far from finished with his praise: "I am so proud of you and so happy to have you working in my company. I know my only child will run it in my spirit when the time comes."

I swallow hard and the guilt I feel towards him almost consumes me. Maybe I should tell him the truth about Noah and our work together.

"Mr. McCarter suggested we have dinner."

"You and him?"

"Yes." I step closer to the kitchen island and place my hands

35

on it. "Do you think that's a ... well ... good idea?"

I'm certainly not going to tell my dad that Noah really wants to go on a date.

"Well," he replies, thinking about Noah's supposed suggestion. "There's nothing wrong with dinner. I've gone out to dinner with my agent many times."

"But?" I hear myself shouting inside. My father has a 'but', and probably a damn good one.

"You're a beautiful woman, Cara," he says. "The most beautiful woman in the world."

"Daddy!" I scold. "Don't let Mom hear that."

"Your mom knows," he replies with a grin. "My little girl is the prettiest in my eyes. But what I will say is that you are a beautiful woman, twenty-two years old and therefore his age."

"What are you getting at?" I feel uncomfortable.

"My point is that maybe a different relationship will develop between you and him..."

"Dad!" I look at him indignantly. "I'm not like that!"

"Cara," he says, sighing, "if you like him, it will come naturally. And that could affect your professional relationship. Both positively and negatively. Your mother has been my most important advisor over the years. No matter how much I threw down the throat of the guys in my management. I always asked your mom first."

"He wants to have dinner with me, not propose."

I roll my eyes and my father grins. "I just wanted to have dinner with your mom and then I married her."

"And how many years in between?"

"Five!"

"So," I conclude. "I have all the time in the world."

"Cara," he says, getting serious again. "You can go out with him and celebrate a business deal with him. But he's still your client. Of course, something unplanned can always happen, but I think you know what I mean."

"Okay," I say, nodding. "Thanks, Dad."

"Anytime," he replies, sipping his espresso. "I'll be in the basement working out."

It's unbelievable that he still values exercise after so many years. At twenty-two, I'm already too lazy to work out.

"Okay," I say. "I'll get back to Mr. McCarter."

"Great" Dad puts the empty cup in the dishwasher and leaves me alone.

I walk out of the kitchen in the opposite direction and up the stairs to my room. On the way, I pull my cell phone out of my purse and open the chat with Marina.

Cara: He's my client!!!

I push open my bedroom door, put my purse on the small stool next to the door, and sit down on the couch. There I reach for my MacBook to open my e-mail program.

Marina: Who?
Cara: The guy from the bar!!! Noah!!!
Marina: The hottie with the fork?
Cara: Yeah!

I roll my eyes at her comment about the fork. She'll tease me about that forever. I'm sure of it. My cell phone rings and Marina's name comes up.

"Hello," I answer, grinning.

"Oh my God!" she screams without a greeting. "Is he as hot as he was in the bar? Who is he? What's he doing?"

"Marina," I sigh. "Calm down."

"I can't," she whines. "You totally screwed up with him and now he's back. It's fate!"

"Oh God," I groan, running my fingers through my hair, "you're crazy. And to answer your question. He's Noah McCarter, quarterback of the Boston Foxes."

"Holy shit," she gasps, "wow, how did that go?"

"Well," I huff, sinking deeper into my couch. "He'll only work with me if I go out with him."

"On a date?"

"Yes," I groan.

"Oh wow," she says, actually speechless. This hardly ever happens. Marina always has something to say. But this time she is silent. I am very surprised.

"Have you said yes yet?" she wants to know, and I roll my eyes. Of course, that's all she's interested in and not the fact that going out with him would get me in trouble.

"I'm not dating my future client," I reply indignantly. "I can't. It's unprofessional."

"What if it works out?" she tries again.

"Marina," I warn. "Please."

"Okay, okay," she backs down. "You really want him as a client?"

"Yes," I say. "I don't think this meeting is a good idea."

"On the other hand," she says, and I know what's coming. Marina is going to convince me to go on a date with Noah after all. "What do you have to lose? If he doesn't become your client afterwards, okay. And if the date sucks, that's okay too. Just look at it as a chance to meet a hot guy and get a new, your first, client."

"Marina," I mutter. "Why did I call you?"

"Because I'm your best friend, you love me, and I only want what's best for you."

"Probably," I chuckle. "I'll send him an e-mail."

"How formal," she mumbles, and I laugh.

"Of course it's formal," I insist. "I want to keep it formal. I don't want him to think I'm interested in him."

"Which, of course, you aren't," she replies with a laugh. "I get it. Write him an e-mail and play hard to get. It's sexy."

"I don't want to be sexy; I want to be professional."

"You're not one to make things simple," she scolds, and I roll my eyes. "Try it and go out with the hot guy. I bet the sex with him is amazing."

This comment is also typical of Marina. I'm not interested in sex with Noah. Why should I be? What would I gain by having sex with him? That's right. Nothing at all.

"Cara?" she asks, "Are you still there?"

"Sure," I reply hastily. "I need to get in touch with him, yeah?"

"Of course," she giggles, "I'll see you around, yeah?"

"Yep," I say and hang up. I save myself the goodbye and reach for my MacBook. I set it on my lap and open my e-mail program.

To: *Noah McCarter*
From: *Cara Catherine Corse*
Subject: *Collaboration*

Dear Mr. McCarter,
I would love to talk again about working together.
Sincerely,
Cara Catherine Corse
Corse Sports Management

Satisfied, I send the e-mail and want to sit back and relax, but my eyes are constantly glued to the screen in front of me. I keep reminding myself not to reload the program. Every child knows that a new e-mail will appear immediately.

Am I starting to lose it? Probably.

Suddenly a new e-mail appears. Much faster than I thought. I frantically grab the device.

To: *Cara Catherine Corse*
From: *Noah McCarter*
Subject: RE: *Collaboration*

Hi Cara,
When are you free? I'll make a reservation for us at Venus.
Noah

I blink. That's his response? He doesn't even begin to answer my message, but directly states that he's making a reservation? At the most expensive restaurant in town, crawling with photographers?

To: *Noah McCarter*
From: *Cara Catherine Corse*
Subject: RE: RE: *Collaboration*

Hi Mr. McCarter,
Please let me know if you're willing to discuss the upcoming collaboration further.
Cara Catherine Corse
Corse Sports Management

I send the e-mail and place the MacBook on the table in front of me. Then I go to my closet to pick out a comfortable sweat suit for the evening. But I don't get very far because my e-mail program stops me again. Stupid as I am, I turn on my heel and hurry back. I flop down on the couch and reach for my laptop.

Touchdowns & Temptations

To: *Cara Catherine Corse*
From: *Noah McCarter*
Subject: *Date!*

The subject line says how important my e-mail is!
Here is my number so you can reach me.
+1 66 8888888
Noah

I puff out my cheeks and don't know whether to laugh or cry. Noah is so rude and kind of cute at the same time. He wants this so much, but I can't just casually text him. Grinning, I start typing another e-mail.

To: *Noah McCarter*
From: *Cara Catherine Corse*
Subject: *Thank you*

Thanks for the number, but unfortunately, I left my work cell phone at the office today.
Have a great evening.
Cara

I'm more than curious to see how he responds.

When my phone beeps - and not my e-mail program - I reach for it. At first, I think Marina or a friend has written to me, but when an unlisted number appears on the screen, I have a different feeling.

My first thought about who it belongs to is confirmed by the message preview on the lock screen.

My heart races and I tap the message with trembling fingers.

41

+1 66 8888888: *That's the number!*

Grinning, I type a reply.

Cara: *That's harassment!*
Noah: *Not when all I can think about is you!*

I open my mouth and close it again when the damn thing in my hand rings. He's calling!

5

NOAH

Getting Cara's private cell phone number was a piece of cake. After leaving her office, I knew I had to meet this woman.

She is amazing.

Not only is Cara incredibly good-looking, intelligent, and works in my industry - which she knows inside and out because of her father, so she will understand my tight schedule. No, she's also funny and sweet. At first, I tried to get the receptionist to give me her number, but she was tight-lipped. Then it occurred to me that she must have contacts in Boston NFL circles because of her father. And bingo! Several of my teammates sent me her number. Of course, I was skeptical that it might be the wrong one. Guys like to make fun of those things, but when our tight end Toby Carson sent me the same number, I was sure it was right. Toby and Cara grew up together. His dad and her dad played together for the Boston Foxes in the 1990s.

Now I'm sitting on my couch, excited as a schoolboy, waiting for her to take my call. The phone rings twice more before her voice comes out.

"Hello," she whispers, "Noah?"

"Hey," I reply. "I'm glad you answered."

"Did I have a choice?" she asks, and I have to laugh.

Actually, she didn't. After all, it's still date versus cooperation.

"No, I didn't," Cara answers the question herself.

"How are you?" I ask instead of answering her nagging.

"Fine, and you?" she asks, and I smile.

"I'm good too. And it's great that you've agreed so quickly."

"Nothing's agreed yet!" She snorts, and I grin. It's going to be very, very fun with her, I'm sure. I just can't believe that she's not interested in me at all, as she's trying to make me believe. After all, she has accepted the conversation.

"No?" I ask provocatively. "Why not?"

"You know why," she hisses. "You're taking advantage of the fact that I want you as a client and blackmailing me with a date."

"I'm blackmailing you?" I laugh again. "Don't you think you're exaggerating? I want the date, yes. Why don't you see it as a quid pro quo that you're going to make a lot of money with me soon?"

Cara mumbles something I don't understand.

"What?" I want to know.

"I said it doesn't work like that," she repeats, "you're crazy."

"Is that how you talk to all your clients or future clients?" I ask, getting up from the couch to get a drink of water. "Because then I can tell you that your career is not going to be a success."

"My career," she mumbles. "I don't think you care that much about my career. You want to go out with me and brag about it."

Now I have to laugh again and go back to the couch. "Let's put it this way," I consider. "There are bigger fish to fry."

"Noah!" I can see that she is struggling for words. She wants me as a client, I know it. And she knows I want to take advantage of that. We are in a pact situation. "Can you be serious for once? Can't you see that this will only cause problems?"

I cluck my tongue and shake my head. For me, there are no problems if we don't look for them. We go out together and we both get what we want.

"No," I say. "To be honest, I don't see a problem. Do you?"

"Of course I do!" she shouts. "I see problems everywhere. I want to do a good job and you ... you only think about yourself."

I sit down on the couch and groan in annoyance. This woman really seems to take everything I say the wrong way. Everything, really, but how can that be? She must realize that this date isn't the worst idea. We could get to know each other better.

"Aren't you at all interested in getting to know the person you are about to work with?" I try again.

"Of course, but I..."

My goodness! It really can't be that she finds another excuse. She wants it too.

"Is that a woman's thing?" I ask. "That you always find a 'but'."

"No, but..."

"You see!" I shoot back. "Once again, you find a 'but'. 'But this, but that.'"

"It's not about my 'but', it's about your ulterior motives."

"I have no ulterior motives."

"Please," Cara replies, laughing gleefully. "Of course, you have no ulterior motives, which is why your first suggestion is a date without even giving me a chance to act as your new agent. Not a serious business dinner, no, a date is what Mr. McCarter wants."

"Shall we call it a business lunch?" I ask. "Would that make you feel better?"

"Yes!" I laugh and she snorts. "I mean, no, I..."

"You what?"

"You're confusing me," Cara mumbles.

The fact that men confuse women is really new to me. I actually think that it's the opposite, that women confuse men and I bet Cara is especially good at it. She's getting more and more interesting.

"I'm confusing you?" I ask. "Why?"

"Because you want to go out with me."

"That confuses you?" I ask and am now really at a loss as to what she wants from me. She's unbelievable. Does she have no idea what effect she has on a man? Hardly, otherwise she wouldn't react like this.

"You're amazing, Cara Catherine Corse," I say.

"Noah," she keeps moaning. "I can't. I really can't and I don't want you to say that."

"Say what?" I ask. "That you're amazing and that I want to go out with you? That's just the truth. Do you get asked out so rarely that you're already uncomfortable with my courtship?"

I hear her breathing heavily. I wait, listening to her erratic breathing. I can't imagine that a woman like Cara would be uncomfortable being asked out on a date.

"You're not going to give up, are you?" she wants to know, avoiding my question.

"What if I say I no longer want you as a client? Then you won't have any leverage."

I let her question run through my mind. She wants me too much as a client to turn me down. That's why this question is nonsense.

Still, if I don't have that leverage, I'll have to come up with something new to ask her. I think back and forth until I find the solution to the puzzle. If she rejects me, we're back to square one. Besides, she has no leverage because we can't work together. That's Cara's current reason for not going on a date.

"Actually, that would be the best thing that could happen to us, wouldn't it?" I say and Cara laughs.

"Excuse me?" she repeats. "You... you can't mean that."

"If we didn't have a business relationship, nothing would stand in the way of our personal relationship. Our problems would be solved."

"Relationship?" she asks, confused. "No one is talking about a relationship."

"My god, Cara!" I groan, rolling my eyes. Does she have to weigh every word I say? I didn't mean a relationship like a 'couple'. Friendships are relationships in their own way, aren't they? "Of course we're still talking about a date. And of course, I still want to be advised by the best agent."

"Idiot," she giggles, "but you still won't get me on a date."

I puff out my cheeks and groan in annoyance. This can't be true. "Don't you want to try it to see if you like it?" I tease. "What kind of sportsmanship is that?"

"I don't have any sportsmanship," she replies promptly. "I hate sports."

"Really?" What is she talking about? You can't hate sports with that body. "I don't think so. You don't hate sports."

"Yes," she insists. "I sucked at sports in school. Do you really think it's better now?"

"How can you compare PE ³to sports?" I ask. "I thought school sports sucked too."

"You're a quarterback," Cara replies, and I hear something rustle. "Sports are your life."

"Football is my life," I correct her. "You can't compare shitty games like dodgeball to football."

"For me, it's all sport," she sighs and rustles again.

"What are you doing?" I want to know.

---

3 Stands for Physical Education. Refers to a school subject focused on developing physical fitness.

"I'm trying to open a bag of potato chips," she answers. "I feel like it." I can't help but laugh. I just have to laugh. "Why are you laughing?"

"Well," I mumble. "Usually women like you..."

"Women like me?" she immediately cuts me off. I press my lips together, hoping I didn't put my foot in it again.

"What are women like me like?" Cara asks. The bag rustles again and then she smacks her lips.

"Women like you go to the gym all the time, eat only salad, and watch their figure."

"When am I supposed to do that?" she asks, amused. "That's impossible. I have a full-time job and a social life."

I have to laugh again. Every word she says makes me like her more. Cara doesn't exercise, doesn't eat salad, and seems to enjoy life to the fullest. I like to splurge on food too, but I usually have to pull myself together. It's okay on birthdays, Thanksgiving and Christmas, but the rest of the time I stick to my diet plan. Lots of fruits, vegetables and nutritious foods. In professional sports, sweets and fast food are not welcome.

"You don't have time to eat healthy?"

"Well," Cara sighs and I hear her sit down again. "If you're looking for a woman who likes to exercise, watches what she eats and generally gives up everything good, you've come to the wrong place."

"Are you flirting with me now, Cara Catherine Corse?" I ask mischievously.

"No," she says promptly. "I'm just telling you that I'm not who you think I am."

"I'd like to meet you so I can see for myself what you're like," I reply. "Maybe over dinner."

"You're really stubborn, aren't you?"

"Always at your service, my lady," I reply with a laugh. "So? Tomorrow night? At seven. I'll pick you up."

Putting all my eggs in one basket and scheduling our date seems to make the most sense to me. Otherwise, she'll be squirming around for hours or even days.

"Noah!" Cara wants to moan again and I roll my eyes in annoyance. On the other hand, there's no point in forcing her to go on a date. It's important to me that she wants to go out with me as much as I want to go out with her. Unfortunately, that's not the case at all.

"That's okay. You don't want to, I understand," I give up. "I have to hang up now."

As if I had summoned him, Alex enters our apartment and quietly greets me. "Alex has come home."

"Alex?" she asks immediately. "Which Alex?"

"My brother," I answer, getting up from the couch. I go to Alex in the kitchen, who looks at me with interest. He smiles at me and opens the refrigerator to take out the carton of eggs.

"Your brother?" she asks again.

"Cara," I mumble and sit down on one of the stools at the counter. Alex looks at me with a grin and takes a pan out of the bottom drawer. "What do you know about me?"

"Not much," she answers. "Your name, your job, your salary and your bank balance, and the fact that you're harassing me and trying to blackmail me into a date."

She makes me laugh again. She must know that under normal circumstances I would never consider hiring her as an agent again. Alex raises his eyebrows and pours oil into the hot pan. I wave him off and signal that I'll explain everything to him later.

"That's not much indeed," I agree with Cara. "And are you sure you don't want to know more? I'm really interesting."

Alex laughs and I throw an apple at him, but as a running back he catches it easily with one hand.

"Of course you are!" Cara clicks her tongue. "Let me know

if you want me to represent you or not. Bye, Noah."

"Cara, wait, I want..."

Tuuuut.

I take the phone out of my ear and stare at the screen. She hung up. This can't be true, can it? I raise my head and look at Alex.

"Hung up?" he asks amusedly, licking his lips. "Looks like Cara Catherine Corse is immune to the McCarter charm."

"Asshole," I grumble, stroking my head. "She's really cool, and I want to get to know her."

"Do you have a crush?"

I roll my eyes. I just think Cara is nice. There's nothing wrong with that, right? Alex meets women all the time.

Because you're not like that, says the little angel on my shoulder and I grimace.

Alex is certainly the bigger womanizer of the three of us. He had a girlfriend for over two years in high school. Daisy. But after she dumped him because she didn't want to share her life with a budding football player, he changed completely. One-night stands and casual affairs have been on his agenda ever since. I don't blame him, because I'm no better when it comes to committed relationships. But I get laid a lot less than he does. Our mother now wonders why she gave birth to three boys, including twins, when she still doesn't have any grandchildren in sight. But I don't see Alex and I as having any obligation in that regard. What do we have a big brother for? Logan should start.

"Noah?" he asks again. "Do you have a crush on her?"

"No," I answer firmly. "I just think she's nice."

"Good luck," he says, winking at me. "Toby said Cara generally keeps her hands off the players." I look at him, annoyed. "Especially the quarterback."

I don't believe him. Alex is just trying to make me feel better about the whole thing.

6

CARA

I can't get the phone call with Noah out of my head. It remains a mystery to me why he wants to go out with me so badly. What does he expect to get out of it? He doesn't really believe that I would consider a relationship with a professional athlete.

I don't want to end up like my mom. Always alone and waiting for football not to come first. Of course my dad loves us more than anything and without his job and career we wouldn't have much. But I often wished he would have come to my school plays or my graduation. Instead, he was usually at the other end of the country playing football.

Life with a famous father is not always easy. I didn't have many friends at school because they often tried to get free tickets to a Boston Foxes game through me. Also, they would always ask me about my dad and were more interested in him than me. One of my ex-boyfriends, Marco, actually managed to talk to my dad the whole time at a dinner with my parents, completely ignoring my mom and me. My dad was flattered, of course, but I thought it was just awful. The next day I ended things with Marco. He said it was okay with him because he wanted to get to know my dad, and he did. And it usually was like this. Once they found out that my dad was Michael Corse, ex-quarterback of the Boston Foxes, they were blown away. More than once, my date knew all of my dad's stats by heart. It's not really something you want to hear on a date night.

"Ms. Corse?" My assistant, Katie, pokes her head through the door and smiles at me. "Do you have time for a quick chat?"

"Yes," I say, pushing my phone aside. I have to stop thinking about Noah and what might happen between us. Because nothing is going to happen. At least nothing serious. There's no question that he's hot, and with his broad shoulders, ripped muscles, and blond hair, he's exactly my type.

"Is this an official appointment? I'm a little distracted." I look at Katie and she shakes her head.

"You don't have your first appointment for another hour. Mr. McCarter wants to see you now."

Katie grins at me meaningfully.

"Noah's here?" I ask.

"No." Katie shakes her head. "His brother Alexander."

I dimly remember Noah mentioning his brother during our phone call and I was shocked at how little I knew about him.

"And what does he want?" I ask hesitantly.

"I think he wants to work with us, don't you?" Katie looks at me as if she can't believe I'm asking.

"Hm." I tilt my head. "Let him in."

Katie nods with a smile and I straighten up at my desk, clasping my hands nervously. This can't be happening; I am meeting Noah's brother. My resolution was to have nothing more to do with McCarter. I don't care which one.

"She's ready," Katie says. I jump at the sound of his voice. It's not his brother, it's Noah. He told Katie he was Alexander because he knew I'd have him thrown out immediately if he wasn't. But since I always look for the good in people, including Noah, I wait. My heart begins to race as his footsteps approach.

"Hello," he says, and I open my eyes.

This is Noah as he lives and breathes!

With brown hair, but this is Noah!

Stunned, I squint my eyes to express my displeasure.

"I'm Alexander McCarter or Alex. Nice to meet you, Ms. Corse."

He offers me his hand in a friendly manner. But I don't take it.

"Are you kidding me?" I snap at him. "You're Noah!"

"I'm..." He stumbles, visibly shocked that his cover has been blown after only a few seconds. "You think I'm Noah?"

"I know it," I answer confidently and cross my arms over my chest. He has to get up early to fuck with me. I know that Noah will try anything to get a date with me, but pretending to be his brother is a really strong move. Does he think I won't notice?

"What are you doing?" I ask.

"I'm not Noah," he continues, insisting on his identity. "I am Alex. His brother."

"Do you think I'll go out with you like this?" I ask. "Pretending to be someone else? How stupid do you think I am?"

Noah looks at me and licks his lips. Then he puts his hands on his hips and laughs. This asshole is laughing at me. This can't be true. He's trying to betray me and gain access to my office in the most despicable way, and now he's laughing too. Unbelievable.

"For the daughter of our legend, you don't know much about the club."

He looks at me amused.

"I'm a sports agent, not a Boston Foxes fan," I say.

"You're Corse's daughter! You must be a Boston Foxes

fan," he sniffs.

He looks almost horrified and I really start to think that this isn't Noah. Noah wouldn't react like this. He would flirt directly and this guy... his brother... He does nothing of the sort.

"Not really," I repeat. "And who the hell are you?"

"So, you don't think I'm Noah anymore?" he asks with a grin.

"No," I answer curtly. "So?"

"I'm still Alex," he says, holding out his hand. "Noah's brother."

"Noah's brother," I murmur and take his hand. "You look frighteningly ... similar."

My eyes sweep over the man in front of me. The same blue eyes. The only difference is the color of his hair. But I have to admit that Noah is slimmer and, in my opinion, much better trained.

"We're twins," Alex solves the mystery. "Identical twins, to be exact."

My eyes get huge.

"Twins?" I blurt out, running my fingers through my hair. "Holy shit, you're identical twins. I can't believe it. You're..."

"Identical twins," he repeats my words. "Just because you say it over and over again doesn't change anything. How can you not know that?"

Alex raises his eyebrows skeptically. I shrug and continue to study him. They look incredibly alike, but the longer I look at him, the more I like Noah.

"Maybe you don't look so much alike," I think aloud, rubbing my chin with my finger. "The hair, the eyes, the lips, but ... Noah is kind of..." I can't find the right words.

"Smaller? Weaker?" Alex suggests.

"Hotter!" I blurt out, covering my mouth with my hand.

Ashamed, I look away and try to make light of the situation

by randomly reaching for my documents. I definitely shouldn't have said that.

"Hotter?" Alex echoes and takes a step towards my desk. He puts his hands on the tabletop and leans over to me. "So why are you torturing the poor guy?"

"What?" I gasp.

"You heard me," he replies. "Noah asked you out."

"Stop!" I raise my hand to stop him and shake my head vehemently. "He blackmailed me, told me I could go out with him or forget about working with him. There's a difference."

"He asked you and looked at the possibilities to get you to do it. I see it more as a kind of leveling the playing field."

"Leveling the playing field?" I ask, raising my eyebrows. "You're a funny guy."

"Thanks," he says with a grin and straightens up. "So? What's it going to be? Are you going to give my brother a chance?"

I know even less about Alex's performance than I did about Noah's yesterday. Both his meeting with me and the phone call afterwards. These brothers seem to have absolutely no scruples or inhibitions when they want something.

"It's really sweet of you to stand up for Noah, but no," I decline this offer as well. "I don't date football players."

"Why?" he asks promptly and I tilt my head back.

"It's none of your business!"

"I think it is my business when it comes to my brother's happiness," he replies. "Noah and I are identical twins, we're soul mates. Let me tell you how deep that goes. We went to different colleges. He went to Georgia and I went to Utah. He got hurt and at that very moment I felt pain in the same place."

"That's bullshit!" I hiss. "Are you kidding me?"

"Maybe," he says with a grin, making me smile. Even though I don't want to admit it ... he is funny. Damn it. I can't find Alex sympathetic. That might influence my decision. A nice family makes my plans not to date a football player falter. Because I really like being with my family.

"What I want to say is this: When he's uncomfortable, I'm uncomfortable. We have a special bond."

"And let me guess," I sigh. "If I hurt Noah, I indirectly hurt you, too, and you can't let that happen?"

"Exactly!" Alex winks and points at me. "And now you're going to give him a chance, right?"

"No!"

"No?" he asks. "How can you be such a hard nut to crack?"

Alex is very entertaining; I have to admit. "Do you do this often?" I ask. "To get women?"

"Not anymore," he answers honestly. "We're getting older."

"Okay." I throw my head back with a laugh. "And are you here because you're looking for a new agent?"

"No, no," Alex says, waving his hand. "I'm very happy with my agent and..."

"Am I interrupting?" I flinch violently and Alex spins around to reveal Noah. He's standing in the doorway of my office with Katie. His hands are buried in the pockets of his jeans, his mouth is set in a thin line, and his eyes are narrowed to slits. His eyes dart between Alex and me.

Oh God, this can't be true. Judging by his tight-lipped expression, I think he believes that Alex is hitting on me...

"No!" Alex laughs. "Cara and I were just talking."

And suddenly Noah grins, as if he's struggling to keep his face straight. I feel my tension melt away and am relieved that he's not mad at us. Or should I have been happy that he was? That would be a much better starting point, wouldn't it? Then I'd be rid of him in no time. That's what I want, isn't it? To make Noah angry and to alienate him so that he doesn't want to go out with me anymore.

"I can see that," he says. "Hey!"

"Hey," I reply and Alex looks back and forth between us with a grin. "I'm off," he whispers. "Nice to meet you, pretty lady."

"Get lost," Noah grumbles and Alex slaps his twin on the shoulder. "Oh and Cara?"

"Yeah?"

"Think of the pain." He winks at me and disappears. Noah looks after him and throws his head back.

"Please don't tell me he tried to lull you with our magical twin connection?"

"Uh," I mutter. "Maybe."

I grin at him and he grins back. Noah licks his lips and comes over to me. I'm glad I still have my desk between us and can keep my distance. I look at Noah and think he looks nervous. And he's actually smaller than Alex. Definitely. They're more different than I thought.

"I wanted to talk to you again and apologize for my brother," he says.

"You don't have to apologize for him," I tell him. "He was nice."

"Nice?" Noah turns as if to check on Alex again. "Alex was nice?"

"Yeah," I say. "And funny."

"And funny?" Noah asks, still skeptical. "Was he flirting with you?"

I'm surprised at the question. He should know Alex well enough to know if he was flirting with me, right?

"Would it bother you?"

"Yes!" Surprised by his clear answer, I gasp. "Of course, it bothers me if my brother flirts - and in the worst case, successfully - with the woman I want to go out with."

"He wasn't flirting," I reassure him. "He was standing up

for you."

"Then I must make it clear that I did not instigate this action!"

"No?" I ask with a grin. "He was very … persistent."

"Persistent?"

"Yes!"

"What do you mean, persistent?" he asks. "Did he say anything that would get me in more trouble?"

"No," I wave him off. "He was very charming and said you wanted to go out with me. At first, I thought you were pretending to be him. After that misunderstanding was cleared up, he tried to explain to me the magical connection between twins."

"And?" he asks, looking at me with a sigh. There's a glimmer of hope in his eyes, which I immediately snuff out. "Have my chances of getting a date gone down even further?"

I groan in annoyance and throw my head back. "Noah," I sigh. "My mind is made up."

"Why?" he asks. "When we saw each other in the bar and … and you dropped your fork. Cara there… there was something between us. Give me a chance."

I'm tempted to say he looks desperate, but I don't dare. The man doesn't look desperate, does he? He can have any woman in Boston. He doesn't have to tell me that there was something between us. He should find another woman to do something with.

"No," I say again. "Would you like something else?"

"Please," he sighs. "One date, one evening. Nothing more."

"No," I repeat, resting my fingertips on the tabletop. "I don't go out with football players."

7

NOAH

Talking to Cara was another total flop. She shut down when I tried to change the subject to a date. What does that even mean that she doesn't want to go out with a football player? That's no reason not to give me a chance. Other women are dying to go out with me, and Cara Catherine Corse? Not her, of course.

She doesn't want to go out with a football player. There could be many reasons for that, and on the drive home, my thoughts are constantly turning to why she doesn't want to. She knows the business; she knows the sport and she grew up with it. If there's one woman who knows what's in store for her with a football player by her side, it's Cara. I don't think she's interested in the fame and money either.

She reminds me of Alex's ex-girlfriend Daisy from high school. Neither of them wants to live our lives. But they are the women we want. I enter our apartment and quietly close the door behind me.

"Noah?" Alex calls out and I sigh as I kick off my shoes. "Is that you?"

"Who else?" I reply, rolling my eyes.

"Mom?"

Our parents and our housekeeper Margaret also have a key.

I have to laugh and join him in the living room. Alex is re-laxed on the couch watching TV. When I get to him, he turns it off silently and grins at me. "So?" he asks. "How did it go?"

"Shit," I answer, dropping into one of the chairs. "It totally sucked, actually. She still doesn't want to."

Alex slowly sits up and looks at me questioningly. "She doesn't want to?" he asks. "She likes you. She said she thinks you're hotter than me." Deeply offended, Alex looks at me as if this were a scandal.

"Really?" I want to know and look at him with satisfaction. "She thinks I'm hotter than you? That must have really hurt your ego."

Alex's ego has always been bigger than himself. Every wo-man has to fall at his feet and those who don't are not wor-thy of him. I often wonder if he wouldn't be like this if Daisy hadn't left him.

They were the dream couple of the school, and I was sure for a long time that she was the love of his life. Logan and our parents thought so, too. After they broke up, Alex was a wreck. Daisy was his first love and broke up with him when it was clear he was going to college in Utah. I liked Daisy, but everyone knew she would never leave Nashville. Alex, on the other hand, held on to the idea that she would change her life for him until the very end. If he had gone to college in Tennessee, like Logan, I'm sure she would have stayed with him, but it quickly became clear that she didn't see a future in the relationship. Daisy called me a lot in the weeks after the breakup, asking how Alex was doing. You could tell she was heartbroken, too. But she had the sense not to get into a long-distance relationship that could have ended in even more chaos.

"Of course," Alex says, laughing. "She's so hot."

"I know," I sigh and sit back. "She said she didn't want to

because I'm a football player." I look at Alex and tug on the waistband of my shorts. "What kind of stupid reason is that? Other women are dying to date a football player and Cara won't?" I shake my head in disbelief. "I don't understand her."

"I've been thinking about that too," Alex says, clasping his hands. "She grew up in these circles. Her father is Michael Corse. Maybe some rookie took advantage of her once. A relationship with her will open some doors for you. There are also black sheep who don't have honest intentions."

I look at my brother for a long time. I hadn't thought about that yet. But it would make sense. Everyone around the Foxes tries to get in touch with Corse somehow, because he's the head of the club. Dating his daughter must be the jackpot for many.

"And now you think she doesn't see any honest intentions behind my efforts because she thinks I'm trying to get to her father?"

Alex nods and I growl.

"What kind of idiots did she date?" I think aloud. "She's amazing and the man who gets her will be more than lucky. Getting Corse would never have occurred to me."

"Maybe she's bad in bed," my brother speculates as the second best reason. Typical Alex. The conversation immediately turns to sex. "She's ashamed that she can't keep up with you."

He waggles his eyebrows in a clearly ambiguous way.

"You're such an idiot," I reply. "You know that?"

"Yes," he says. "But it could be."

"I don't think so," I answer immediately. "I think the thing with her father is a good approach."

Cara won't be convinced by me anytime soon. Meanwhile, I don't know what else to do.

"This sucks," I groan. "I meet a woman I'm really interested in and she hates me."

"You could change jobs," this idiot suggests. "After all, football is an existentially important part of your life."

"Great," I grumble, throwing my hands in the air and standing up. I paced up and down. Alex watches me, but doesn't say anything. He seems quiet and equally at a loss. And when he's at a loss, it's really serious. He always has some advice for me, or at least a stupid remark.

"You could show her your university degree in economics," is his next brilliant idea.

"Idiot," I grumble. "That won't change her mind as long as I'm playing football."

"You didn't take the advice to stop playing either."

"No!" I look at him, annoyed. "Do you have any useful suggestions?" I lean against the back of the chair.

"You have to keep at it," he says clearly now. "You have to prove to her that you're serious and that you really want to get to know her. But you also have to ask yourself if it's worth it."

"Of course it's worth it," I snap at him. "Could you take the whole thing more seriously?"

Alex doesn't seem to understand that I'm really interested in Cara. If I just wanted to get her into bed once, I wouldn't make such a fuss.

"I'm taking this seriously," he replies. "But I also don't want you to get your hopes up."

"Hm," I say. "I'm not. I just want to get to know her. That's all."

Alex raises his eyebrows and grins.

"It's really sad that you don't want to have sex with this woman," he says suddenly.

"Of course I want to have sex with Cara." He grins and I groan in annoyance. "Don't change the subject. Please, Alex."

"First of all, you could work with her, right? Do you have a contract?"

I nod. Cara has given me a contract to become a client of Corse Sports Management, though not entirely voluntarily. Knowing full well how important it is for her resume and the company's client list.

"Yes, but she's not thrilled," I say immediately. "Cara doesn't really want me as a client anymore. She's only doing it because she knows it will help her resume."

"Understandable," Alex says. "She's not interested in you and wants to keep you at arm's length so she can stick to her own resolutions."

"Why is she making it so unnecessarily complicated?"

"Because she's a woman."

I roll my eyes and go to the kitchen to get a drink. I don't think she's making it so complicated just because she's a woman. Cara doesn't want to date me because of my job, and I have to find out why. And then I have to work against it. I'd be laughing if I couldn't get to my date, right? She wants to go out with me, I know that. Sooner or later my job won't be an obstacle for her either.

"Do you want a drink?" I ask and Alex shakes his head. "Do you think she'll pass you on to another agent at Corse Sport Management?"

"No," I say honestly and walk back to Alex with a bottle of water in my hand. "She wants the glory of representing me way too much for that. Cara is ambitious, very ambitious, and she wants to prove to herself, to me, and I'm sure to her father, that she can advise me. She won't give me up, but she will keep our contact to a minimum."

"Does that mean she will only communicate with you by e-mail?"

I nod and run my fingers through my hair. "If anything. Maybe I'll put her out of my mind after all."

"You're giving up?" Alex looks at me with wide eyes.

63

"Seriously? Why?"

"Cara's stubborn, really stubborn, and she won't back down."

"And you're a McCarter," he retorts, punching me in the chest. "Noah, you'll get it. You always get what you want. You wanted to be a starting quarterback in Boston, and you got it. You wanted to go to college in Georgia because they had the best quarterback prospects, and you got it. So, you're going to date Cara Catherine Corse."

I sigh and look at him.

"Maybe you're right," I agree. "I can't give up."

"Good!" Alex gets up from the couch. "Shall we go for a drink?" I look at him and nod. Why not? It can't hurt to take your mind off things for a while. "I'm going to take a shower," I answer. "See you in a bit."

"Are you driving?"

"Uber?" I suggest, and Alex frowns. He hates Uber. He always thinks the drivers take a longer route just to spy on us when they recognize us. They force us into conversations and want to take pictures. I'm more relaxed about it. We live this privileged life and play football for a lot of money. You can talk to the fans and take pictures with them.

"Come on"

"But if it's a fan, you have to talk to him."

I roll my eyes and nod.

"That's fine," I reply. "I'll talk to him."

★★★

Alex and I stand in the street waiting for our Uber.

"He's late," Alex says, and I roll my eyes. We haven't even waited two minutes. For Alex, everyone has to be on time; otherwise, he gets offended.

"He'll come." I kick at a stone flying across the road and look at him. Hopefully, the evening will distract me a bit and I won't have to think about Cara all the time. What she's doing tonight and why she rejected me. I don't understand. At least she can give me the chance to get to know each other. Maybe after a date we'll realize that we're not right for each other. As a couple, I mean, and we become friends. That's worth something, right?

"Noah?" Alex grins at me and shoves his phone back into his jeans. "Get her out of your head."

"I wasn't..."

"Of course you were thinking about Cara," he sighs. "And I didn't go out this evening to listen to your heartbreak over and over again."

"I'm not heartbroken," I brush it off. "I don't understand it. But it's not heartbreak, you should know that. After all, I'm still eating."

Alex stopped eating after Daisy left. The guy was so out of it, we thought he was going to give up his scholarship.

"Anything you want to tell me?" As always, when the subject turns to Daisy, he goes on the offensive. Even after all these years, it still bothers him that she left him.

"The Uber's here," I dodge, and he starts to protest, but unfortunately the car actually pulls up at that moment. "Let's get in."

Alex gives me an angry look that shows the topic hasn't been forgotten. He can't stand the fact that even after almost seven years I'm still talking about how he was so out of line because of Daisy.

The Uber stops in front of us and the man at the wheel rolls down the passenger window. "Noah Carter?" he asks, looking at us.

"That's me," I reply. "We're going downtown."

"Get in," he says. "I've got another user we're picking up a few blocks away."

Alex rolls his eyes in annoyance and circles the car to get in behind the man. I sit next to him in the passenger seat to keep my promise. When the man starts to drive away and I look at him to give him the exact address, his jaw drops. "Oh my God," he screams. Yes, he screams like a girl. "You ... you're Noah McCarter, our ... our quarterback, and you ... you ..." He looks in the rearview mirror. "You're Alexander McCarter. I got the McCarter twins in the car."

He becomes more and more agitated, but fortunately manages to start the car and drive off. He spends the next twenty minutes telling us what a big fan he is. He doesn't even notice that Alex isn't listening to him. My brother keeps looking at his cell phone.

"Our last passenger is waiting." The man stops and rolls down the passenger window again. "Corse?" he asks and my head spins. "Cara Corse?"

Now Alex seems no longer interested in his cell phone.

"Yes," Cara says, coming closer. "Noah?" she asks, not answering the driver. "What are you doing in my Uber?"

"What are you doing in my Uber?" I reply with a grin and unbuckle my seatbelt to get out. Cara takes a step back as I open the door and join her on the street. I couldn't be that lucky to run into her here of all places, could I?

"Noah!" Alex calls. "Get in. We have to keep going."

"Hey, Alex!" Cara looks past me and waves to my brother, who has unbuckled his seatbelt to peer between the two front seats.

"Are you coming with us?"

"I'm going home," she says.

"Home?" I ask softly, looking over my shoulder at the driver. Yes, he's nice, and I don't think he'd hurt Cara, but I still

66

don't like the idea of her taking an Uber or a cab. I don't have a good feeling about it.

"And you take an Uber? What about your car?" I ask.

"I've been drinking wine," she replies.

"But Uber?" Yes, my argument is ridiculous. It's admirable that she calls an Uber instead of getting behind the wheel. Unlike me, Cara doesn't see the poor driver as a potential sexual predator. I usually don't either. The woman drives me crazy. "Next time, call me. Where's your car?"

Cara looks at me questioningly and turns her head. She points to a black Mercedes SUV. First the Ferrari, now the Mercedes. Not bad. I wonder how many cars she has. Now this is a conversation that doesn't end in a fight.

"Keys?" I hold out my hand. "I'll drive you home in your car."

"No?"

"Yes!" I turn and look into the Uber. "I'll drive her home and then catch up in a cab."

"What?" Alex and the driver ask out of the same mouth.

"Get back in the car now," my brother says, annoyed. "Both of you. We have to go."

But my mind is made up. Tonight, I'll drive Cara home and take the opportunity to finally find out more about her.

I repeat again, "I'm driving Cara home," and smile at her. Of course she shows no reaction. "Don't worry. I'll pay you anyway," I turn to the driver.

I want to pull my wallet out of my jeans and pay for Cara's ride, but Alex shakes his head. "I'll do it," he says. "You drive."

I nod gratefully to my brother and push the door shut. Then I turn to Cara.

She has her arms crossed over her chest and looks at me with anything but enthusiasm. "Did you really just do that?" she asks as the Uber pulls away. "I ordered an Uber."

"And I'm not letting you take an Uber tonight or tomorrow because your car is here." I point to her Mercedes SUV.

I start to walk away, but Cara makes no move to follow me.

"Are you coming?" I ask.

"What are you doing?" she hisses. "I've taken Ubers so many times and nothing's ever happened to me. You should have gone with your brother."

"But I don't want you in a car with a strange man." She raises her eyebrows and laughs. Okay, that does sound strange.

"And who are you?" she wants to know. "Not a strange man?"

"At least not that strange, right?"

"Hm," Cara says and sighs.

"Keys?" I hold out my hand and make a request for her to give me the keys. Cara is annoyed, but opens her purse to rummage through the huge thing and finally finds the key.

"Here," she says, handing it to me. "But don't you dare make the slightest dent in it."

"Sure," I reply and she struts past me to her car.

She looks really hot in that skimpy dress that barely covers her cute butt. I follow her, whistling.

"And don't you dare whistle at me again," she shouts without turning around.

8

CARA

I'm starting to think that Noah McCarter is stalking me. Even though that's completely ridiculous. It was a coincidence that he and Alex were in the same Uber as the one I ordered to take me home. It's amazing how often I run into the McCarter twins these days, and I know for a fact that one of them wants to go out with me. And now he's going to drive me home. I must be completely crazy. Everything we're doing here is doing absolutely nothing to help me keep my resolution, and it's not helping us build a purely professional relationship with each other. Which we're not doing, just because he has my personal cell phone number. Our working relationship is not official yet. We're still waiting for his lawyer to review the contract. Once Noah is my client, he will no longer drive me home. That's unprofessional.

Noah opens the car door, and the headlights come on. They shine at us, illuminating his face in that orange glow that makes me grin.

"What's so funny?" he asks, opening the driver's door. With a heavy heart, I walk to the passenger side of my car. I hate it when other people drive my cars.

"The orange of the headlights flatters your face."

Noah laughs and adjusts the seat, then the rearview mirror.

"Don't pretend," I say, looking at him. "I hate that."

"Excuse me for being at least eight inches taller than you," he says, rolling his eyes. "No one can sit here."

"I didn't force you to drive me."

"I know," he admits, turning on the engine with the start button. It roars to life and he grips the leather-covered steering wheel. I buckle up and watch him. To be honest, Noah looks pretty damn good in my car. He's wearing a black V-neck t-shirt that accentuates his muscular chest and a pair of jeans. He's either not wearing a jacket because it's still very warm or he left it in the Uber.

The car rolls away and he steers it onto the street. I look away from him and out the window.

"Can you put in the address?" he asks, and I look at him again. "I don't know where you live."

"Sure," I say absentmindedly and he smiles at me. "Sorry." I tap my saved address called 'Home' and press 'Start'.

Noah looks at the navigation system and opens his mouth when he sees the area. "You have your own villa?" he asks. "Wow."

"No," I mumble, crossing my fingers because it makes me a little uncomfortable in front of him that I still live with my parents. But it's the best solution so far. I'm looking for a place of my own. I hope Noah didn't think I was going to invite him over for drink so he could have sex with me. He can forget it. Not only because of my parents.

"I live with my parents. The house is huge. But I'm looking for an apartment."

"Okay," he says, smiling. "You're very close, aren't you?"

"My parents and I?" I ask, glad for the small talk. The thought of us keeping quiet all the way home drives me crazy.

"Yes," Noah says. "Your parents and you."

"Yes," I answer with a smile. "I'm their only child and, of

course, we're close. I love being with them and I'm glad we all live in Boston now. Still, I'd like to have my own place."

"I understand that." He grins and leans back. My Mercedes is an automatic, and Noah casually rests his right arm on the center console and steers the car through the dense Boston traffic with his left hand. God, he's so insanely sexy. I'm really tempted to imagine this happening more often now. Him at the wheel and me as his girl next to him. We could drive to his place together, or he'd drive me home. I quickly look away.

"Alex and I see our parents very rarely."

"You're from Tennessee, right?"

"Yes." He grins. "A real country boy." Noah winks at me. "You think that's sexy?"

"You in a plaid shirt with a lasso in your hand and cows next to you?"

"I was thinking more of a guitar and a campfire," he replies. "But if you like cows and lassos better." Noah looks at me and I shake my head, laughing. Still, I have to admit that he would certainly look good in a plaid shirt. "I'm flexible, honestly."

"What's life like there?" I ask. "A normal family, a small, cozy house with just enough rooms for everyone?" The words just flow out of my mouth, but I'm really interested. All I know is villas, endless luxury and a family that never had time. My parents love me, I know that, but they were very busy. I don't have any brothers or sisters, so I was often alone. Since Mom and Dad came from normal backgrounds, I occasionally observed those normal families at my grandmother's house in New Jersey. But I never played with the children. It never happened, and my grandmother didn't want to spend all the time she had with me on playgrounds.

"Life in Tennessee?" he asks. "It's monotonous. Everybody knows everybody."

"Hm," I say.

"No caviar and yachts and villas. No private jets and designer clothes."

"Are you making fun of me?" I ask and he shakes his head.

"No. I'm sorry. For me and Alex, this is all we've ever wanted. We can give our parents so much, but, of course, I understand that it's different when you've always had everything. We didn't walk around in plaid shirts and cowboy boots and lassos, that's bullshit."

"Too bad." I grin. "That would have been something."

Noah wiggles his eyebrows and I laugh again. "Those are all bad rumors about us."

"Then tell me the truth," I say. "I'm very curious."

"Okay," he says. "I grew up in a suburb of Nashville. It was almost its own little town. We had grocery stores, gas stations, high schools." I listen with interest. "Alex and I have another brother. Logan is five years older."

"Another brother?"

"Yes." He grins. "My mom hoped so much with us twins that we'd be a girl and a boy."

"And then she had three boys?"

"Yes," Noah answers. "My parents didn't know our genders. Alex is two minutes older than me. He was originally going to be called Alexandra because Mom was pretty sure he was a girl."

"And you, Noah?"

"Yes," he says. "They had a boy's name and a girl's name ready. Without further ado, they changed Alexandra to Alexander."

"That's funny," I laugh. "And Logan was excited about his brothers?"

"Not at all," he says. "He found us mostly annoying and unnecessary."

"I always wanted a sister, but unfortunately I never got

one," I tell him. "Pregnancy with me was very difficult for my mother."

"I'm sorry," he says, smiling at me. "Sometimes I really want to hit Alex against the wall, but to live without him? Impossible."

"Because of your special bond as twins?" I giggle and Noah laughs.

"We've always been together. In kindergarten, at school, and then we were separated for college, which was hard."

"I believe you, but now you're back together. And you live together, right?"

"Yes. We live in an apartment, but it gives us enough space so we each have our privacy." Noah looks at me and winks. What does that mean? Is he indirectly telling me that I can come over? Absolutely not.

"And what does your brother do?"

"Logan?" I nod. "He's a tight end for the Nashville Warriors."

"You're lying!" I say it faster than I meant to. My hand lands on his muscular upper arm and I pull it back as quickly as if I'd burned my paws. I shouldn't have touched him. That was a big mistake. Touching his muscular shoulder and feeling the warm skin under my fingers ...

"I mean I... you're all... uh... football players?"

"All of us!" Noah laughs. "Alex and I used to imitate Logan."

"With success." I grin. "And who's the best?"

"Logan's been playing a lot longer than us," he says, smiling. "He's won the Super Bowl twice. We haven't yet." I nod and keep listening to him. "My stats are better than my brothers', but there's more competition at their positions. I'm sure you know from your dad that it's easier to set records as a quarterback. But I don't think I'll ever be able to match him.

He was amazing."

I turn away and look out the window. He was bound to mention my dad and his accomplishments sooner or later. They all do. My dad, the superstar, the Boston Foxes legend, and them, the young players who want to date his daughter.

"Cara?" Noah asks quietly. "Are you okay?"

"Hm," I mumble, but don't look at him again. Hopefully, we'll get there soon. I want to get out of the car.

"Okay," he says. "You seem ... so ... so different."

Of course, I'm different when he - like all the other guys - raves about my father.

"Did I say something wrong?" he keeps asking.

"No," I snap, running my fingers through my hair, "everything's fine."

"That's nonsense," he replies. "We had a great conversation, for the first time, mind you, and now you're completely shutting down. What have I done?"

"What they all do eventually," I hiss. "Tell me how much you adore my father."

Noah flinches and slams on the brakes uncontrollably. We both jerk forward and he stops. He hits the hazard lights and looks at me. What the hell is this? He's just supposed to drive me home, that's all. It's enough that I was stupid enough to get into a conversation with him in the first place and then have him in my car.

"What?" asks Noah, confused. "You're mad because I mentioned your dad?"

"I'm mad because you're just like all the other boys," I reply. "First, they act like they're interested in me, and just when I think maybe I should reach out to you and enjoy the conversation, you tell me about my dad's stats. I know he's thrown five hundred and seventy touchdown passes and I know he's thrown for 50,656 career passing yards, more than anyone before him and currently active. I also know that he's been an MVP six times and won the Super Bowl five times in his career. He's the greatest quarterback of all time and..."

"And I didn't know all that," he cuts me off.

"What?"

"I don't know the exact numbers," Noah says, smiling. He takes my hand and strokes the back of it with his thumb. My skin tingles and I bite my lip. That's what they all say - that they don't know the numbers. And when they talk to my dad for the first time, they can rattle off all his accomplishments.

"Everybody says that."

"I'm not everyone," he says, looking at me. "Cara... I want to get to know you, and I ... I didn't realize that you ... you don't want to because ... because you think people are only interested in your dad." I take a deep breath and let it out. "I'm sorry you think that. But I am ... I'm only interested in you."

"Noah, I..." I turn away from him and lick my lips. "I can't."

"Why not?" he asks. "I also promise I won't memorize your dad's passing yards or the years of his Super Bowl wins."

"1994, 1995, 1997, 1999, when my mom was very pregnant, and again in 2001."

"You really know all the statistics," Noah says, and I have to laugh.

"I'm his daughter. I need to know."

"Probably," he mumbles. "I want to get to know you, not your dad. Do you believe me?"

"Yes," I say, pulling away from him. He leaves me and retreats as well. I am grateful that he understands that I need distance.

"But that's not the only reason. Can you please drive me home?" Noah looks at me again and wants to say something back, but he doesn't. Instead, he puts the car in drive and drives off. "Do you want me to call you a cab?" I ask. "I'll pay for it, of course."

"No need," he replies, setting the indicator for our neighborhood. "I can do it myself."

"Noah!" My voice sounds pathetic and I look over at him. His features are hard and his eyes are fixed on the road. He's angry with me. "I'm paying for this and-"

"You don't have to pay me for a cab, I can just about afford it," he says ironically. "Give me the code to your gate." He rolls down the driver's side window and looks at me immediately.

"220599"

"Okay," he replies and hands it over. "Your birthday, isn't it?"

"Yes," I say in astonishment. "How did you figure that out?"

"You told me that your mother was very pregnant at the Super Bowl in 1999. So, you must have been born shortly after that." I look at him, speechless, because I didn't think he was listening to me that well. "Yes, I'm listening to you."

My cheeks heat up as Noah pulls up the driveway and parks the car behind my mom's Porsche.

"You can keep the car," I say, looking at him. "Drive it home and bring it by my office tomorrow." And again, the words come out of my mouth faster than my brain can sort them out. I don't want him to keep my car and have a reason to see me again. Even if only at the office.

"Okay?" Noah sounds skeptical. "Thanks, that's nice."

"It's the least I can do after ruining your evening with your brother."

"You didn't," he assures me, leaning over the center console and grinning at me. "I'd rather have spent half an hour in the car with you than two hours in this bar with my brother and the boys."

He grins. "All right," he says, coming closer to me. "You need to get out."

"I know," I mumble. "Good night."

My heart beats wildly in my chest as our eyes meet again. Tense, I bite my lip, waiting for him to wish me good night too, but he doesn't.

"Get out, Cara!" he demands, looking exhausted. He even closes his eyes and I can see that his left hand is gripping the steering wheel tightly.

"Why?"

"Because I don't want to kiss you on your doorstep and have your parents find out," he admits. Still, I can see how much he wants to. The air in the car is tense to the breaking point. I lick my lips again. Whether it's out of nervousness or because I'm turned on, I don't know. Noah is unbelievably attractive and my type.

Without wanting to, I lean forward to him. So close that his breath hits my face.

"Noah?" I ask. "Kiss me."

"Cara, no!" He pulls away from me. As far as he can into the car. He even leans his head against the driver's side window. Embarrassed, I pull away as well. He has rejected me. Fuck. I quickly open the passenger door.

"See you later," I mumble and stumble out of the car. "Give my assistant the keys."

"You know we shouldn't, not like that," he says, and I shake my head, slam the door shut and run to the house. The engine of the Mercedes roars behind me and Noah leaves the property in it.

9

NOAH

The next morning, I drive Cara's Mercedes to practice to return it to her at noon. I notice the questioning looks of my teammates, but I don't pay any attention to them. It's none of their business that I'm driving Cara's car. After what happened last night and what she told me, she's still not interested in getting to know me. Still not, even though she wanted to kiss me. I heard her desire clearly. More than that. My body tingled and I saw myself at the destination of my dreams. Well, almost, because sometimes dreams are just dreams. Fuck! No one wants their parents watching their first kiss, right?

It would have been my chance to feel her beautiful lips on mine. To kiss them and taste them just once. But I was stupid enough to turn her down.

Have I completely lost my mind?

I think so, definitely. This can't be true. There's the woman I've been chasing for days, who I've been trying to get to go out with me, who asks me for a kiss, and I have nothing better to do than turn her down? It doesn't get any dumber than that.

I've probably wasted my only chance to get close to Cara. I open the trunk and take out my gym bag. My eyes fall on Cara's travel bag, which is also inside, and I can't help but smile. Sighing, I shoulder my bag and close the trunk. After the way I behaved yesterday, I'm further away from my destination than ever before.

Alex peppered me with so many questions this morning that I felt like I was being cross-examined by the FBI. My brother wanted to know every last detail and called me stupid when I confessed that I didn't want to kiss Cara. My motives were completely unknown to Alex.

"Noah!" Toby, our tight end and my source for Cara's number, approaches me. "Hey!"

"Hey!" I reply and join him. "You're alright?"

"Yeah, you good?"

"Yep," I reply. "I can't complain."

"New car?" he asks as we walk together and at first, I don't know what to say. I can't believe he didn't recognize the car. They've been friends too long and too well for that. I can't help but be interested in how good of friends they are. If there was ever more than friendship between them.

My stomach clenches and I press my lips together to keep from making an inappropriate sound.

"No," I say as calmly as I can. "This is Cara's Mercedes."

Silence falls between us and Toby exhales.

"Cara?" He laughs. "Cara Catherine Corse?"

"You know another one?" I ask slightly irritated and he rolls his eyes.

"No, but why do you have Cara's car?" he asks, turning to look at the car again.

"I drove her home last night and she left the car with me," I explain. "I'll get it back to her, don't worry."

"I'm not worried about the car," he replies with a wink. "It's nice that you two get along and she's giving you a chance."

"Yeah," I mumble. "She's still not giving me a chance. She doesn't want to date football players, she says."

"I don't think Cara wants to date anyone in general," Toby

interjects. "She's extremely paranoid that every guy is only interested in her dad and not her."

"She told me that too," I say, not sure if I should tell him more. Yes, they are friends and get along well, but I don't want to discuss Cara's secrets and problems with him. She won't like it. "She doesn't like to be told about her dad, but she knows all the statistics herself," I say after a few seconds.

"That's typical of Cara," Toby replies amused. "She's Michael's biggest fan and really knows every statistic, but as soon as a guy knows anything about him, she sees red."

It's strange to hear Toby talk so intimately about Cara and her family. If I didn't know better, I'd say there's another feeling rising up inside of me. Is it jealousy? I hope not. That would be bad, because then I'd be more involved than I wanted to be.

"Do you know why?" I ask, holding the door to the training building open for him.

"Not really," he says. "I know she had some guys who promised her the moon and then shot her down as soon as they met her father and took a picture with him. High society in New York and Boston isn't so high anymore when it comes to sports legends. Her dad is the greatest of them all."

"Oh wow," I reply, entering the locker room and going to my locker. "So, what am I supposed to do?"

Toby shrugs.

I sigh and open my locker to change.

"Give her time," he advises me with a smile on his face. "Make friends with her and prove to her that you're not interested in Michael."

"Hm," I say, getting out of my jeans. "I hope this works."

"Definitely," he says, winking at me. "She'll fall for your charm."

"What charm?" asks Alex, stepping up to the locker next to mine. "He doesn't have any."

"But you do?" Toby replies belligerently. "Half the women who go to bed with you only want to screw a football player once."

"So what?" Totally unimpressed, Alex shrugs. "We all get something out of it, right?"

"Of course," Toby says. "We've all seen your dick in every state at least once."

I ignore their friendly banter and continue to change. Pants, pads and Jersey until I'm finally ready and reach for my helmet. I can't get Toby's words out of my head. Not even when I step onto the field and warm up. Cara probably doesn't want me to leave my thoughts today until I'm back with her. It's just a shame that I'm stuck here for at least another three hours of practice.

★★★

I enter the Corse Sports Management building and head straight for the elevators. I know Cara told me to leave the key with her assistant, but I don't want to miss the chance to see her. I push the button to call the elevator. To my surprise, it opens immediately and I get in. Smiling, I go to the third floor, where Cara's office is, and lean against the wall. Then I pull my cell phone out of my pocket and open her chat.

Noah: Are you in the office?

The blue checkmark that indicates the message has been read and three dots appear immediately. I wonder if someone was waiting for my message and wants to see me. I'm probably telling myself that. Cara's main concern is her car.

Cara: Yeah, and you? Is my car still alive?

I grin and type a reply as the elevator stops on the third floor and the doors open.

*Noah: I hit a bump this morning before practice.

I can't help but grin as I get out of the car and make my way to her office. Several angry messages from Cara arrive immediately.

*Cara: ???
*Cara: I hope you're kidding?
*Cara: Are you crazy?
*Cara: Noah?!
*Cara: Answer me!
*Noah: How am I supposed to answer you calmly when you harassing me like this?

Her assistant is sitting at her desk, just like yesterday, and I approach her.

"Hello," I greet her, "I'm here to see Mrs. Corse."

She nods with a smile and stands up. "Just a moment," she replies pleasantly. "If you could take a seat?" She points to the waiting area with two black chairs and a small table between them. To be honest, I don't think I need to sit there. Cara's waiting for me, and since she thinks I've wrecked her car, even more so.

"Who do my tired eyes see?" I turn around and Michael Corse comes up to me. We've met before at the stadium, before the Foxes signed me. I was watching Alex then. I'd be lying if I said he wasn't one of my sporting idols. "Noah McCarter."

"Good afternoon, sir," I clear my throat and shake his hand. "Nice to meet you."

"The pleasure is all mine," he says, putting his hands on his hips. "You played well last season. I'm glad we brought you in."

I am flattered by his appreciation. It was also the right decision for me to come to Boston. If only for the chance to play with my brother. "Thank you very much. I'm very happy to hear that."

"With you on the team, we'll bring the Super Bowl back to Boston," he says without putting any pressure on me. "Have you settled in well?"

"Yes," I answer. "It hasn't been difficult for me. I've liked the city for a long time."

"You should," he replies with a smile. "Boston is quickly becoming a home. I know what I'm talking about. In the years I've been elsewhere and my wife and Cara have been here, I've missed them and the city terribly."

I believe him immediately. I missed my family during college, too.

"Noah!" Cara's voice makes me jump and I turn to face her. The bright summer dress with the colorful floral pattern hugs her slender body perfectly. The decorative bow at her bust makes it look sexier than it really is. Cara's hair is tied back in a ponytail, with a few strands hanging down. "Hey, Dad," she greets her father.

"Hello, darling!" Michael walks up to her and kisses her on the cheek. "Do you have an appointment?"

"Yes," she says, "I didn't even know you two had a meeting."

Cara's gaze meets mine and something flashes in her eyes that doesn't bode well. Oh God, she thinks I actually wanted to meet her dad.

"It was a coincidence!" I say, hoping she'll believe me. Of course, in a way, I admire her father. What this man has done for football is unattainable. Still, I don't put getting to know her above that. "We met in the hallway."

"Hm." Cara doesn't look convinced, but she smiles. "Will you come into my office?"

"Sure," I say and nod to her father. "Goodbye, sir."

"Goodbye," he says. "And have a good game this weekend. The opening game can sometimes make or break a whole season."

If he was trying to encourage me, he definitely needs to practice that again. The only thing he's managed is to make me even more nervous. It's my first game as the starting quarterback for the Boston Foxes.

"You're scaring him," Cara turns to him and looks at me. "He'll get through it."

"We'll see," Michael replies, smiling at us. "See you on Sunday."

"See you on Sunday," I mumble and follow Cara into the office. She closes the door behind us and raises her eyebrows.

"He started the conversation," I defend myself again. "You have to believe me and he said that I..."

"I know," she cuts me off. "He's a big fan of yours."

She smiles at me and walks past me to her desk.

"Really?" I ask and Cara nods.

"He really is," she says. "He likes the way you play and thinks you'll bring the Foxes back to greatness."

Speechless, I look at her, waiting for her to burst out laughing and tell me she's kidding, but she doesn't.

"Really?" I ask again. "He thinks that of me? Wow."

Cara shrugs, unimpressed, and crosses her arms over her chest. Of course, she immediately gets defensive when you gush about her dad for too long. Crap. This is exactly what I promised myself I wouldn't do.

"What about my car?" she asks, changing the subject. Her

eyes pierce me and I can't help but grin. I casually walk toward her.

"Let's talk about my talent again," I tease her.

"Stop the bullshit," she hisses. "What about my car? If you broke it, then..."

Now I'm standing right in front of her, looking down at her. Cara stops her sentence and looks back at me. If I take another step forward, I can lean in close enough to touch her lips. We are so close. Her breath hits my neck because, despite her high heels, she is much smaller than me. The blood rushes through my veins and I have to be careful it doesn't go to my dick. This woman is pure temptation.

"Then?" I resume our conversation, struggling to concentrate.

"Then God have mercy on you," she hisses and I have to grin.

"Don't worry," I say and cluck my tongue. I place my hands on either side of her as she leans against her desk. Cara looks back at me and I lean closer to her. This time I'm not as stupid as I was yesterday. I want this woman. "There's nothing wrong with your car."

"Oh, really?" she asks, slipping under my arms. "I want to see it."

"Where are you going?"

"To see my car," she says, grabbing her bag. "Are you coming?" I look at her, still confused.

"You want me to come with you?" I ask. At the risk of losing my chance with her again, I want to hear her say it.

"If you don't want to..." Cara lets the sentence hang in the air. "You won't get another invitation to visit Boston."

I don't think I've ever taken off so fast.

10

CARA

It's been a long time since I've seen Marina. She has brought me new ultrasound pictures and is telling me all about her pregnancy.

"I don't see anything," I say, holding the ultrasound photos up to the light. "Are you sure it's a boy?"

You really can't see anything on this picture. Especially not the little line that is supposed to be a penis.

"She can't say for sure until the next appointment, but we think it's a boy," my best friend proudly reports.

"But I wanted a girl," I grumble, which makes her laugh.

"Me too," she replies, "but Caleb is very excited about having a son."

"I'm sure he is," I mutter. It was so obvious that a man like Caleb would want an heir, a firstborn. Whether the child is healthy or not is probably irrelevant.

In the end, I still hope it's the right decision for my best friend and that she won't regret being with him one day.

"We are very happy," Marina continues as my phone vibrates and I look at it.

+ 1 new message from Noah

Out of respect for my friend, I don't answer it. I stay focused on our conversation, which is anything but easy for me. My fingers itch to see what he has written. Last week I went to the opening game with my parents and saw him win. We also met up once to explore Boston, and then he went to his first road game in Seattle. Unfortunately, the Boston Foxes lost the game. Noah was pretty frustrated.

To be honest, I don't know how I got into this whole thing. But suddenly he's so present in my life, and I think we could really be friends. My embarrassing request for a kiss is long forgotten, and I've been very careful not to get close to him since. I want to try to build a real friendship with him.

"And you?" asks Marina, sipping her water. "How are things going with Noah?"

That brings the subject back to him. Doesn't she have anything more to say about the baby?

Apparently not.

Marina knows there's nothing going on between us. But she keeps asking me about him. It's like a long, annoying record.

"There's nothing going on with Noah," I reply, annoyed. "We're friends."

"Who says my question is on a sexual level?"

"Everyone who knows you," I reply matter-of-factly.

"Okay," she says, grinning at me. "How's your friendship going?"

Maybe I'll just tell Marina what she wants to hear and that'll be the end of it. But that's not right. Noah and I are friends. She shouldn't read more into it.

In her eyes, Noah is the absolute jackpot for me.

"Good," I say. "Our friendship is good. We do a lot together."

"And?"

"And what?" I ask skeptically.

"Damn, Cara." Marina rolls her eyes. "You're not telling me you have a purely platonic friendship with this really hot guy, are you?"

I don't think it's that far-fetched that we're friends. Noah and I get along well and have the same interests. We both like fast cars, love to shove greasy pizza down our throats, and enjoy the same comedy shows on TV. Outside of work, he's good for me. It's nice to spend time with someone who likes football but doesn't talk about it or my dad all the time.

"Actually, yes," I reply. "Why don't you believe me?"

"Because in my eyes it's complete nonsense."

"In your eyes?" I ask, raising my eyebrows. "Why can't you leave me alone?"

As soon as I say it, I bite my lip. Shit, I didn't want to say it like that. I didn't want to blame her. I know she doesn't begrudge me.

"You think I am judging you?" she hisses. Since she got pregnant, she has become much more sensitive. Things she used to laugh about are now big drama. I always manage to say something that upsets her, or worse, makes her cry.

"No!" I yell. "I never meant to say that."

"Really?" she asks pointedly.

"Yes," I reply. "I didn't mean it." I take a deep breath and close my eyes for a moment, catching myself and becoming aware of my words. "It's complicated."

"What?" she asks, picking at her salad. "That you're dating the hottest guy in Boston and..."

"I really want to be friends with him."

Marina sighs and raises her eyebrows.

"What's the problem? Why don't you just fuck him?" She's dead serious and looks at me, completely calm again.

"That's not what you asked, is it?" I reply annoyed. "I don't want anything from Noah. Not like that."

"I didn't say you should marry him," she says. "I know your principles, but damn it..." Marina tries to calm down, which makes me giggle. The subject of Noah McCarter is really getting her blood pumping. I chuckle again.

"What does Caleb think about you being so interested in Noah?"

Now she rolls her eyes.

"You're deflecting, Cara," she replies. "It doesn't matter what Caleb thinks."

"No?" I ask and she shakes her head.

"No."

In my opinion, Caleb would go crazy if he knew. I always had hope that she would find a better man, but since she got pregnant, I've buried that hope forever.

"Noah McCarter is so hot. Please sleep with him just once."

She couldn't have said it any clearer.

"Forget it," I refuse. "That just makes it unnecessarily complicated. And what makes you think I even want to?"

"Every woman wants him," she says succinctly. "And there's no better position than yours to end up in the sack with such a hot guy."

"You're annoying! Can we please talk about something else?"

My phone screen lights up again and I glance over. Marina is grinning across the table. "Noah?" she wants to know sweetly. "You're welcome to answer him."

"No," I say. "I'm here with you."

"So what?" she says, "Will you at least introduce me to him soon?"

"Why?"

"Because I'm your best friend and I want to meet him."

"You know him," I correct her request. "And I really hate to remind you how you totally embarrassed me in front of him."

I still blush when I think of that evening. It was so embarrassing.

"Oh, that!" Marina shakes her head. "I was happy to do it. You should thank me."

"You're terrible," I hiss. "And I don't know if your condition makes it worse."

She laughs and drinks her water.

"I'm your best friend and you love me," she finishes my sentence.

"That too," I say conciliatory. "But you're being really mean right now."

"Guilty and..." Marina stops and looks at the door. "Your man just walked in the door with another guy."

"What?" My head spins around and sure enough, Noah and Alex enter the restaurant. "He didn't say he was going to lunch."

"No?" Marina asks and I give her an annoyed look. "And I thought that was what friends did."

"Oh, you know..." I have an insult on the tip of my tongue, but I save it. Marina is deliberately provoking me because she wants me to comment on the fact that Noah and I are more than friends.

I look at him again and start to watch him when Alex sees me. He raises his hand and I do the same. Then he nudges his brother and points at me. Noah's face lights up and he smiles too. My smile widens even more as they make their way to our table.

"Uh, they're coming over here," Marina comments.

"Shut up," I hiss.

"Hey," Alex says and sits down in the chair next to Marina so that Noah sits next to me. Alex grins at me and turns to my best friend. "Alexander, hi, but Alex is fine too. You were with Cara when Noah met her at the bar."

Why does he stress that Noah met me there? Well, that's what happened. Noah came to our table and, with Marina's active assistance, approached me.

"I am Marina. Cara's best friend and her guilty conscience." I roll my eyes and the guys laugh.

"I'm Noah," he introduces himself and shakes her hand. "Nice to meet you."

"Nice to meet you, too," she says, grinning at me. Before she can say any more stupid things, a waitress comes to our table.

"Hi," she says, aggressively flirting with the McCarter twins. And how could it be otherwise? Alex jumps up.

"Hi," he says. "What can you recommend?"

Noah moans beside me and I grin.

"We have the chicken burger with sweet potato fries on the menu today. But I think you'd both prefer something healthier."

She giggles artificially and I roll my eyes. It's pathetic for our species.

"I think I'm allowed to sin today," Alex flirts unabashedly and now even Marina rolls her eyes.

"Okay, and what about you? Do you sin too?" she turns to Noah. I look at her and notice that she has noticed my glance. How can you be so pathetic, first making eyes at Alex and now at Noah? I'm not jealous, but it's unbelievable how some women behave. I clear my throat and pick up my glass. Noah looks at me. Marina laughs.

"Maybe you'll order something to drink first..." my best friend says, saving the day. "They'll order food when you get back. You should check the menu first."

To emphasize her words, she pushes Alex towards ours.

"And what would you like to drink?" the waitress asks much more reservedly. Still, she bats her eyelashes as she looks back and forth between the twins. She must be beginning to realize that she's annoying.

"I'll have a Diet Coke," Alex says, and Noah nods at his brother.

"Me too, thanks, and if you have it, I'd be happy to add a carafe of water."

"Of course," she purrs, "as you wish."

Then she finally turns and disappears, hips swaying at the counter, to pass on our order. Noah reaches past me for the menu and grins at me.

"And what can you recommend?" he wants to know.

"If you think I'm going to recommend something sinful," I say. "Forget it. My baked potato was very good." I point to my empty plate.

"Okay," he says. "Then I'll have one."

Alex studies the menu for a moment, but sticks with the snappy waitress's suggestion. She returns far too quickly for my liking.

"Here I am again," she whispers, and this time I deliberately roll my eyes. "Here you go," she says, placing a drink in front of Alex and Noah. "Did you choose what you want to eat?" She tucks the tray under her armpit and pulls an iPad out of the pouch on her belt to type in the orders.

"The baked potato for me," Noah says.

"Spicy or regular?"

"Regular," he says, and she nods and looks at Alex.

"I'll stick with the burger. Medium rare, please, and regular fries."

"Sure," she replies and walks away. I shake my head again and Marina rolls her eyes.

"Why are you looking me like that?" asks Alex. "I think she's nice."

"Of course you do," Marina says, not hiding the irony in

her voice. "You like her."

"Maybe," he says, and we all laugh. Noah also lifts his Diet Coke and with it the coaster, because the wet glass is sticking to it. A piece of paper with a phone number on it appears from underneath. My chest rises and falls tensely and I try not to show how annoyed I am by the situation. I mean, the fact that she's shamelessly flirting with them is okay, I guess. But giving Noah her number when I'm sitting next to him is really bold.

I'm not jealous, I don't think, but I still don't like the idea of him contacting her later. I'm worried about him now. As his friend.

"She gave you her number?" Alex asks, gasping for breath. At least he's as horrified as I am by this brazenness. "That can't be right. I put so much effort into flirting with her and you get her number." Annoyed, he throws his napkin on the table and Noah laughs.

I take it back! The guy is just upset that his twin got the number and not him. Wow, this afternoon has reached a new low.

"Here!" Noah tosses him the note. "You can have it. She won't know the difference tonight anyway."

Marina bursts out laughing and I stare at the twins, stunned. This is unbelievable. What a cheap shot. On the other hand, Noah is right. She won't be able to tell them apart tonight, and she probably doesn't care who she goes to bed with. Still, I don't like the fact that it was originally Noah who got the note and not Alex. Marina takes the note from Alex.

"She wrote it neatly," she says.

"It's not easy to write a number on a napkin," I say sarcastically, and everyone looks at me with wide eyes. Especially Noah. His eyebrows rise slowly. "What?"

"You're not jealous, are you?" he asks with a grin.

"Please!" I gasp. "Jealous? Me?" I point at myself. "In your dreams!"

A huge grin appears on Noah's lips, and he leans over to me. I want to pull away, but he doesn't let me. Instead, his hot breath hits my face. A shiver runs down my spine and I bite my lip. Don't give in, Cara.

"In my dreams?" he whispers.

"Hm," I mumble, unable to make another move.

"I dream about winning the Super Bowl," he replies and I stare at him. Noah grins and pulls away. "What did you think?"

He looks at me in amusement and I slap his arm. But this teasing slap quickly turns into a real punch that hits me full force. My palm tingles and my heart beats faster. We both know what he dreams about at night, and I'm not sure it's good for our friendship.

But as long as I don't react and control my heartbeat, everything goes like clockwork.

11

CARA

I'm at the stadium with my parents to watch a Boston Foxes game live. They are playing the Seattle Commanders. Their new quarterback, Jalen Armstrong, just joined the team this year. The Commanders drafted him. My dad raved about him on the car ride and said the Foxes could have gotten him, but they thought Noah was a better option for the future. Rookies, especially quarterbacks, can play worse in their first season in the pros than they did in college, and the Foxes didn't want to take that risk. The number of interceptions is significantly higher in the rookie season in the NFL than in college and later years. The young players have to adjust to the more experienced and often more agile defensive players who play at a different tempo.

I listened patiently to my dad, but I didn't put much stock in what he was saying. He likes to talk about players and how he grades them. Especially quarterbacks, only to realize that they will never be as good as he is. Dad would never say it in public, but he enjoys being the best quarterback ever.

When I'm at the stadium with my parents, we sit in our family box, of course. But, when I'm not with them, I prefer to sit in the stands because I think you get a better feel for the game. Today we are not only here as a family, but also to represent Corse Sports Management.

Although it's mid-September, the East Coast of the United States is still experiencing the uncomfortable heat of late summer. The air in the stadium is stagnant and I fan myself with a flyer to create a breeze.

The stadium is already packed and the atmosphere, as always, is electric.

Noah wrote to me last night. I haven't heard from him today, but he says he's always introverted on game days. He needs the peace and quiet to concentrate better, and who am I to begrudge him that? Nevertheless, I write him a short message wishing him good luck.

Suddenly it gets unbearably loud and I turn my attention to the tunnel where the Boston Foxes players are coming out. Led by Noah, they are running onto the field to warm up. He looks even hotter than usual in his jersey with the pads and the unbelievably tight pants. His helmet dangles loosely in his right hand as Alex nudges him. He raises his finger and points around the stadium. Noah says something to him, shakes his head and speeds up his steps to get away from Alex.

The more I get to know the twins, the more different I find them. Noah is quiet and introverted, while Alex is loud and direct. I wonder who their brother Logan is more like.

"Will you ever get used to the stadium?" my mom asks and I look at her.

"Probably not," I answer with a sigh. "But it's part of our lives."

"It is," she says, "and soon it may be more a part of yours than you realize."

I raise my eyebrows in question, but she just grins at me. It's nonsense that her statement is directed at Noah. Now that I'm working in sports management myself, I'm just less able to push away who I am.

"I'm Michael Corse's daughter," I reply. "Of course it will always be a part of my life."

"I didn't mean your dad," she replies with a smile and looks out at the field. I follow her gaze as Noah puts on his helmet. Suddenly, he raises his hand and waves in our direction. I open my eyes in surprise. Was it meant for me?

"We're on the jumbotron," my mom says, pointing to it. "He's waving at you."

Heat rises inside me, and I barely dare look at the jumbotron. Why is he doing this? And why does my mom think he's waving at me?

"Why do you think he's waving at me?"

"He only waved after you were shown." She shrugs.

So, I wave back, because it's only right. Our names are displayed below our faces: "Dana & Cara Corse - Michael Corse's wife and daughter."

"Great," I grumble. "Now the whole stadium knows we're here and Noah McCarter is waving at me."

"That's nice," she replies.

"Oh, Mom," I mutter. "I don't like being the center of attention."

Which is another reason I'm not going out with Noah!

"I know that," she says with a smile, squeezing my arm. "But he waved at you."

I can only hope that my mom doesn't jump on the same stupid Noah bandwagon as Marina. My best friend has nothing else to talk about. Maybe her pregnancy, but there's not much news about that either, apart from the fact that her belly is growing.

"We know each other," I say. "I work for him, Mom."

"I know that." She smiles at me with satisfaction. "I think he's nice and very handsome."

"Mom!" I look at her indignantly. "Why would you say

that?"

"Because it's the truth," she insists on her point of view. "You don't think so?"

Yeah, great, what can I say now? Of course, Noah is handsome and nice and certainly a dream son-in-law, but not for my mother. She can kiss that goodbye. Noah and I are friends, and that's fine. In the last few weeks, we've become closer and closer friends and I think that's nice. Really nice. "Well, I think... Daddy!" I call, glad that my father's appearance saves me from the situation.

"There you are," he says, smiling at us. "Are you guys excited? I think Noah is going to be in a really good mood today. There's no way he's going to be overshadowed by a rookie."

I look at the field and at Noah. He throws a few balls to Alex and fakes a run. Then my eyes slide over to Jalen Armstrong. He's talking to one of the Seattle Commanders. He looks pretty good; I have to admit. But I hear he has a girlfriend he met in college.

"Hm," I reply. "We'll see."

"Shall we sit down?" My dad points to the chairs in front of us and smiles at us.

"Of course," my mother replies and I follow. Soon after we sit down and the fans take their seats, the spectacle begins. The teams enter and the national anthem is played.

The Foxes have won the coin toss and open the game with their first drive. The offense, led by Noah, takes the field and lines up.

My dad is a bundle of nerves for the next few minutes, and when Boston goes down seven to fourteen with a touchdown after the first quarter, he gets even more tense. Things get better in the second quarter; our defense holds strong and comes up with an interception. Noah comes back on the field and I lean forward. The guys have picked up some yards on the turnover and I hope we can score a quick touchdown.

"Come on," I mutter as they line up and Noah takes his place. He gives the command and the center takes the snap. Noah takes a few steps in the pocket. But a defensive player is there immediately and pulls him down.

"Damn!" I jump up reflexively, earning a quizzical look from my dad. "Sorry."

I quickly sit back down and try to calm down. They are only on their second attempt and still have all the time in the world. On the next drive, they pick up a few more yards. They finally make it into field goal range. Noah's annoyed face is shown on the jumbotron. He removes the safety catch from his helmet, tosses it to the ground, and sits down on the bench. Alex sits down next to him.

I sigh and turn my attention back to the team that now has the advantage: Seattle! Led by their young quarterback Jalen Armstrong, they line up. Granted, he's really, really good. Seattle scores a touchdown. My dad is cursing next to me and the other people in the box are whispering.

I try to block out their voices because most of them are criticizing Noah and questioning him. They think they would have been better off with Jalen. That's total bullshit, and if they thought about it any more, they'd know it. Noah has several years of experience in the league that Jalen Armstrong has yet to gain. Today is just a good day for him, that's all.

"Come on, Noah," I whisper. "Come on."

The offense comes back out onto the field and everything goes back to normal. They line up and the center throws the ball to Noah. Noah runs - in my opinion - the wrong way again and gets knocked down. It's crazy. He can't complete a pass. The worst part is that everyone is happy when it finally goes to the break. Seattle has two touchdowns and a field goal, plus another point lead. And unless miracles happen down there, this is going to be a very humiliating night for the Boston Foxes. My parents go to the box to get more drinks. I stop and look around the stadium. It's my first visit this season and, of course, I want Noah to play better. The whole team should play better and step it up in the second half.

The third quarter starts as bad as the second. Noah's passes are disastrous, and Jalen Armstrong plays like he's a god.

However, our defense miraculously manages to keep the score at 10-28 for a few more possessions.

I look at Noah. His attitude has changed.

He is much more aggressive and his brother notices. Noah pushes him away and gives him a clear command where to stand. Of course, Alex doesn't take this lying down and a verbal exchange ensues between the twins. Noah is able to win this and Alex has to position himself where Noah wants him. This time Noah targets another player and the move works. He gains a few yards.

"Yes," I whisper, biting my lip as they set up again. This time it works and they score a touchdown. The kicker's extra point is right on the money, too. It's still 17-28, but it's a glimmer of hope. On the Seattle Commanders' next drive, our defense doesn't give them a chance, and it's as if Noah's touchdown untied the knot. On top of that, Armstrong throws an interception and the ball comes back to us.

After another touchdown on this drive, the score is 24-28 going into the fourth quarter.

"Oh God," I mutter, running my fingers through my hair. You should never write off a football game before the final quarter. My dad has also gotten up and is giving the boys instructions from his position. I'm so glad he gave up his coaching career for now. Poor guys.

The Boston Foxes have the ball again and line up. Noah has a heated discussion with Toby and walks over to his spot, shaking his head. I clasp my hands together, as if praying will do any good, and stare out at the field. They make it to the end zone on this drive. It's not just me, the whole stadium is tense. If the Foxes score a touchdown now, they will have caught up with Seattle.

"Come on," I whisper as they line up and Noah gets into position. He has to make it. The lines are very tight in front of the end zone, but it's only a few yards away. The center throws the ball to Noah and he goes up the middle. As expected, he is immediately blocked.

"Shit!"

My parents look at me questioningly and I shake my head. As if they weren't thinking the same thing. We have one more try to get the touchdown and finish this drive without losing any points. The team gets back in position. Noah takes the pass and Alex breaks free in the end zone. I jump up and scream as he catches the ball.

"Very good!" I yell so loud that the people below me look up. "Keep it up!"

In the next few minutes, the opposing team passes the Foxes with a touchdown and takes a 35-31 lead. With one minute left on the clock, the Foxes have the ball again. They have to score a touchdown or lose the game. Time doesn't want to run out and, of course, the Commanders call a timeout in the middle of our drive.

I look at Noah. He looks calm, talking to his coach and then to Alex and Toby. I pace up and down in front of the box, trying to get rid of my nervousness.

"Cara?" my mom asks, "Are you nervous?"

"No," I reply. "Not at all."

She grins at me, but I just roll my eyes and concentrate on the game. The timeout is over and the offense lines up again. Noah gives the final instructions to his players and they get into position. The center takes the snap, the ball lands in Noah's hands and he dances in the pocket. This gives the defense time and they take advantage.

The quarterback is tackled.

How in God's name can he run back there? This is a black day for the Foxes. The next offensive drive fizzles out as well and time runs out mercilessly.

★★★

I'm standing in the parking garage waiting for my parents, who are still shaking hundreds of hands. I quickly excused myself by pretending to go to the bathroom and walked on, hoping to meet Noah. Not only did the Boston Foxes lose the game, but they caused a turnover in the final seconds, allowing the Bears to score another touchdown. A really bad Sunday.

"Cara, hey!" I turn to see Toby coming toward me.

"Hey!" Smiling, I walk over to my old childhood friend and give him a hug. "Sorry about the game."

"It's okay," he says with a shrug. "The season's still long and we had a bad day."

"I noticed," I remark. "Who are you playing next week?"

"Atlanta," he says. "Where are your parents?"

"Still shaking hands," I reply with a grin.

Just then the elevator opens and Noah gets out.

He speaks to Alex who follows him. Noah raises his head and looks at me. The corners of his mouth turn up and I smile too. That makes Toby turn around.

"Oh yeah," he says with a grin, waggling his eyebrows. "Of course you're waiting for Noah."

Heat rises in my cheeks and I hastily avoid his gaze.

"Not at all," I contradict half-heartedly. "It's all ... coincidence."

Toby can barely hold back a laugh.

Noah and Alex come over to us, and Toby is kind enough to take a step aside.

"Hey," Noah says, and I smile at him.

"Hi," I say. He leans over and plants a kiss on my cheek.

"How did you like the game?" he wants to know with a grin.

"Hm," I mumble, not quite sure what to say. The game wasn't that good, but I can't say that. It would only bring him down. "It was okay."

"You're a terrible liar," he replies.

"Sorry," I chuckle. "I was trying to cheer you up."

I raise my eyes cautiously, my heart pounding. Noah smiles back at me and pulls me closer. Inevitably, I snuggle up against him and place my hands on his muscular chest.

"What are you doing today?"

I look up at him in surprise.

"I'm waiting for my parents and then we're going home, and you?"

"I want to go home too," he mumbles. "Do you want to come with me? We can cook something and call it a night."

Surprised, I look at him and walk past him to Alex and Toby. I'm not sure if they're paying any attention to us, as they're deep in an animated discussion about the game.

"Alex is flying to Nashville tonight."

"Okay, wow," I mutter. "And you're not?"

"I have a few more appointments in the next few days. I'm flying out on Wednesday."

"Okay," I say again, not very witty, and Noah laughs.

"So, are you coming with me?" he asks.

I bite my lip, asking myself the same question. Noah and I have never been alone at his house to spend an evening together. I think back and forth, undecided. I wonder if this is too intimate. We are friends, but isn't that what friends do?

"Cara?" he asks. "Yes or no?"

"I don't know," I answer honestly. "I don't have my car..."

"I'll drive you home later," he offers. "And, of course, I won't drive you if you want to stay with me."

My pulse races and goose bumps spread over my body. I can't imagine that there could be more between us than just a nice evening with friends. It's not possible.

"Do you have bad intentions towards me?" I try to keep the conversation light.

"Absolutely not," Noah says, winking at me. "We're spending some time together, as friends."

I take a deep breath and look back at Alex and Toby.

"Okay," I finally give in. "I'll come with you."

12

CARA

Noah opens the front door for me and I go in after him. This is the first time I've been in his house. The lower level of the apartment is dominated by a large kitchen. A huge black leather couch sits in the middle of the room, facing a giant flat-screen TV.

"Make yourself at home," Noah says, setting his gym bag down by the stairs. "Wine?"

"Sure," I reply, smiling at him. "My usual wine buddy is unavailable at the moment." He raises his eyebrows, which makes me grin. "Marina," I explain to him. "She's not allowed to drink wine right now."

"Oh, right!" he says. "Is she excited about the baby? How much longer will it be?"

"She's very excited," I answer, following him into the kitchen. "She is due to give birth in February."

I put my purse on the counter and sit down on one of the stools.

"Marina can hardly wait and is counting down the days."

"It's still more than half a year away," Noah replies amusedly, taking two glasses from the cupboard. Then he walks past me into the living room to get a bottle from the huge wine rack on the wall.

"Red or white?" he asks, looking at me over his shoulder.

"White, please," I reply. "That's what I tell Marina, but she doesn't want to hear it. Is this a sweet wine?"

"Like you?" he replies mischievously.

"Sweet?" I ask.

I laugh and Noah sets the bottle down in front of me.

"Of course I'm sweet," I claim. "You have no idea how sweet I am."

"No?" he asks, resting his forearms on the kitchen island and leaning toward me. "Could you show me?"

I lean over the counter to him. Noah looks at me expectantly. His gaze dances between my lips and my eyes. We're so close again, I can feel his breath on me. My heart beats faster and my skin tingles at the thought of his lips on mine. Fuck, we're friends. I hastily pull away, ending the magical moment between us.

"The wine," I clear my throat. Noah stays in his position for a moment and stands up as well.

"Wine," he mumbles. "Of course."

He takes the glasses and pours a glass for each of us. As he pushes the glass toward me over the kitchen island, he makes sure we don't touch. My refusal has offended him. Or so it seems. But we're friends, and friends don't give each other longing looks, do they?

"We were talking about Marina," Noah picks up the conversation again. "How long have you been friends?"

"Ever since we sat next to each other in middle school," I say. "She's basically been my best friend my whole life."

"That's nice," he replies. "Is she also... uh... rich?"

He looks away sheepishly, as if it's an inappropriate question, but it's not. My parents are rich. So, it's not out of the question that I have rich friends.

"No," I say. "Her mother worked as a secretary at our

school. So, Marina and her brothers could go to school for free."

"Oh, wow," Noah says. "Didn't she feel...uh, awkward among all the rich kids?"

"Sometimes," I answer with a shrug. "She didn't really mind. In fact, it spurred Marina on because she wanted to make something of herself. How was school for you?"

"The richest student in our school was the mayor's son. And he was an idiot."

"Did he play football?" I ask with a grin, batting my eyelashes.

"No!" Noah replies indignantly, sipping his wine. "He was on the swim team and always showed off his body."

I can't help but laugh.

"He showed off his body?" I ask. "And what did you do?"

"This masterpiece..." He points to his body. I follow his hand and realize once again how unspeakably handsome he is. Oh yes, he is. The gray t-shirt he's wearing today hugs his chest perfectly. "It's hard work. That idiot didn't work hard enough."

"Well," I say, sipping my wine. "I think swimming is a hard sport. Maybe you could try it?"

"Are you kidding me?" he asks and I laugh.

"Maybe," I reply with a grin. "Is Alex your best friend?" Somehow, I guess he is.

They've been together their whole lives and, if Alex is to be believed, they have this magical relationship.

"Kind of, yeah. My best friend Jamie still lives in Nashville. He took over his dad's company after college."

"You went to school together?"

"Yes," he says. "Our teachers separated Alex and me in high school, and I was put next to Jamie."

"Right," I say. "And how was that for you?"

"I think it was easier for me than it was for Alex. However, at that time he was seated next to Daisy. Shortly after that she was his first girlfriend."

"Oh, how sweet," I squeak.

"Of course you think it's cute," he says. "Daisy and Alex were together for nearly three years."

"Why did they break up?" I ask with interest, sipping at my wine.

It's nice to talk to him about his past and his friends from school. It helps us get to know each other better.

Noah is not someone who brags, I've noticed that by now. He doesn't need to brag about his dad's accomplishments or how many yachts his family owns. Probably none, from the sound of it. He's terribly normal. So is Marina, and that only makes her more interesting to me.

"Daisy didn't want to live the life of a football player's wife," Noah says, twirling his glass in his hand. "Alex was devastated and useless for months. Meanwhile, we thought he wouldn't make it to college, drop his scholarship, and go back to her."

"Oh God!" I clap my hand over my mouth. Still, I find it hard to believe that Alex was seriously heartbroken. On the contrary. He's a total player and philanderer. I bet he'd hit on me, too, if he had the chance. "I can't quite picture Alex heartbroken. Sorry."

A little ashamed of how I feel about his brother, I smile at him.

"Not anymore," Noah says. "Daisy destroyed him completely. He hasn't had a relationship since and doesn't want more than one night, or maybe two if it went really well. He really loved her."

Noah looks at me, and if I didn't know better, I'd say you can still see the pain in his eyes. He seems to care about what happened to his brother.

"It's so beautiful and so sad at the same time," I whisper. "And ... and you? Did you have a ... Daisy?"

Noah looks up and meets my eyes. Goose bumps spread over my body, and my heart starts to beat faster.

"No," he says and I let out a gasp of air. "I didn't, and did you? Did you have an Alex?"

"I don't date football players," I answer and Noah sighs.

"That's not what I meant," he says. "I meant did you have a high school sweetheart?"

"Who hasn't?" I ask him in return.

"Me?"

"Really?" I look at him, confused. "That's not possible."

"Cara," he says emphatically. "Don't change the subject. Did you have one?"

I look at him and sigh.

"Yes," I answer. "I did."

"And?"

"I had a high school sweetheart. That's it."

"Name, age, address," he says. "And what the hell did he do to screw things up with you?"

"Well." Avoiding Noah's gaze, I laugh mirthlessly. I twirl my wine glass in my hand, sloshing the contents back and forth. "He was more interested in my father than me. Like everyone else."

Noah looks at me in surprise, and I raise my eyebrows.

"What?" I ask. "Did you think I was making this up?"

"No?" he replies. "I didn't. But not everyone is like that."

"At least everyone I've met so far," I say, sighing softly. "Not everyone, of course, just like not all women are only interested in your money."

"You, for example," he says.

"Yes, because I have more than enough of it and it's not important to me. I know that's easy to say when you inherit fifty million dollars. As the sole heir, mind you. But I really don't care. I would rather have grown up like you did. My father was never around. He never saw any of my school plays and didn't really know much about my life. Instead of coming to my high school graduation, he had to go to a prep camp in California. Sports always came first, and I don't want that."

Noah can't get a word in as I monologue about my life and my father's role in it.

"I'm sorry," he replies sincerely. "I'm afraid I can't say otherwise."

"No," I say with a sigh, "I'm sorry, we've gotten completely off topic. I had this boyfriend, like I said, and he was fascinated by my dad. At the time I thought it was cool, but eventually I realized it wasn't."

"And that went on and on?" Noah speculates.

"Unfortunately," I answer. "It was always the same. First, they wooed me, I fell for it, and then they told me they wanted to meet my dad."

Noah purses his lips and sighs.

"Is that why you didn't want to go out with me? Because you were afraid I would use your dad to cement my position with the Boston Foxes?"

"No," I say honestly. "I just don't date football players."

"Not at all?" he asks in horror.

"No, not at all, and stop asking me about it. I've already told you several times."

"And what do you do when there's this incredibly handsome, unique and insanely charismatic guy who's also a fantastic kisser?" he asks, taking big steps towards me. "And then he tells you he's a football player?"

Noah keeps looking at me and stands close to me. I have to tilt my head back to meet his gaze.

"Then I tell him I'm not interested."

"Even if you're already in love with him?" he whispers and leans down to me.

My heart is in my throat and I swallow. When exactly did the conversation about Marina's pregnancy, wine and Alex's first girlfriend escalate like this?

I look at Noah and know where he's going with this. Damn it. What am I going to say? He's never going to give up.

"Is this the male hunting instinct?" I blurt out, making him jump.

"Wha... what?" he stammers, and I take advantage of the situation to pull away from him and put some distance between us. He is way too close to me and I can't help but think about kissing him.

"Is it because of some male hunting instinct, that you'll try anything to get me?"

"Male..." Noah laughs and stops. Suddenly he jumps towards me so I can't react quickly. He grabs me and wraps his arm around my waist, pulling me against him. My body bounces against his and I feel his hard muscles. Noah looks down at me and his breathing accelerates.

"Don't do it!" I warn him in a husky voice.

"What?" he asks and leans down to me. My heart is beating faster again and everything in me is resisting to snuggle up to him and let him do what he's about to do. But damn it ... I'm just a woman. And he's an extremely hot guy.

"Don't kiss me," I beg him, looking up at him. "Please."

"Why not?" he whispers. "My god, Cara."

Noah blows air so it brushes my cheek. Goose bumps spread across my body, and I run my hands down his broad chest.

"I should have kissed you earlier," he whispers.

"It would complicate things unnecessarily," I say, looking at him. "And you know that."

Noah meets my gaze and closes his eyelids. I think he already sees it and knows it's not a good idea, but then he cups my face with his big hands. I want to protest again. But I just stand there and stare at him.

"Damn it, Cara," he growls. "This isn't going to work, you know that. We can't just be friends."

His statement echoes in my head and I want to answer him when his lips are already on mine.

13

CARA

The feeling of Noah's lips on mine is insanely good. Much better than I ever imagined and would admit. He gives me time to return the kiss, but I'm unable to react.

My inner voice is still warning me about this kiss and what it will change between us.

I can't let it happen and stumble into the inevitable: Falling in love with Noah McCarter.

But his lips feel too good. They fit perfectly against mine. My hands, resting on his chest, run up and down. Noah moves even closer to me, and his grip on my hips tightens. Slowly but surely, my resistance begins to crumble because it feels too good. From his muscular chest, I work my way up his neck and intertwine my hands.

Finally, I return the kiss.

It breaks down all the walls I have so carefully built.

Noah intensifies the kiss, I give in and let his tongue enter my mouth. His right hand moves to my cheek and pushes into my hair. He tilts my head and I let him, making the kiss even more intense. His face hovers over mine and I let him take control. Our tongues engage in a fierce battle to see who will gain the upper hand. Noah pulls my body closer to his, and I feel his hard member against my stomach. Fuck. I didn't think this kiss would turn him on so much. But, of course, it does, because it feels incredible.

I've been resisting the inevitable for so long, but there's no point anymore. With this kiss he tears down my last walls and I give myself to him.

"What?" he whispers, running his thumb over my cheek.

"Nothing," I say, smiling at him. "Everything's fine."

Our lips meet again. This time the kiss is more passionate. Noah's tongue penetrates deep into my mouth and elicits a moan from me.

Suddenly his hands are on my thighs and he lifts me up, forcing me to wrap my legs around his hips.

"Where are you going?" I ask between kisses as he carries me up the stairs.

"What does it look like?" is his simple reply.

Yes, what does it look like? His bedroom!

Before I can even think about whether we should really do this, he kisses me out of my head again. The top floor of his apartment passes me by like a movie until Noah opens a door and carries me to bed. The sun is setting and is so perfect in the sky that it shines a warm orange through the curtains of the large picture windows.

Noah sets me down in front of his huge bed and smiles at me.

We stare into each other's eyes for a moment. Finally, I reach out and stroke his cheek. Over the shadow of his beard, his beautiful lips that can kiss so sinfully, and a small scar on his left temple that I've never noticed before.

"What happened there?" I ask, touching the scar carefully with my fingers.

"A little fight," he answers. "With Logan."

"You had a fight with your big brother?" I ask and he laughs and kisses my neck.

"Yes. Now let's move on to more important things."

Noah leans towards me again, but I shake my head.

"I think it's important," I counter and push him away.

Noah furrows his eyebrows and doesn't seem to understand what I want from him. His mind is entirely fixated on sex.

"At the risk of you kicking me out," I mutter, letting myself fall back onto the bed. "Tell me about it! Everything! The scar, other scars, your brothers."

Noah opens his mouth and can't believe it at first. I know he wants nothing more than to sleep with me right now. But damn it! This interests me so much more than sex.

"Okay," he admits. "You're killing me, Cara Catherine Corse. Wait a minute."

I'm about to reply when he turns on his heel and disappears into an adjoining room. A few seconds later, he returns, clothes in hand.

"Here," he offers me one of his jerseys. "The door on the right is my bathroom. Go in and change. It might be a little uncomfortable in your jeans."

"You're going to tell me?" I ask in astonishment, crawling off the bed.

"Sure," he says. "If you want to know."

Chuckling, I jump out of bed and disappear into the adjoining bathroom. It's smaller than I expected. Gray tiles, dark gray furniture, and a huge round tub line it. The windows are floor-to-ceiling and covered with opaque pleated shades. I take off my jeans and shirt and place them on the edge of the tub. Then I slip into the jersey. It comes up to my knees. The Boston Foxes logo is emblazoned on my left chest. A big 'B' with the outline of a fox's head around it. Without thinking about what I'm doing, I lift the fabric and hold it up to my nose. To my disappointment, it doesn't smell like Noah, but like lavender detergent. But what do I expect from a fresh Jersey? I turn around once to look at my back. It says 'N. McCarter – 10' in big letters.

This day ended very differently than I had imagined. And now I'm lying in his bed, albeit in a completely vegetative state. Grinning, I look at myself again and tie up my hair on the way back to the bedroom.

Noah is sitting on his bed. His back is against the big headboard, and he's looking down at his cell phone. I clear my throat to make myself heard.

"Here I am again."

He has swapped his gray t-shirt for a white one and his long sweatpants for shorts.

"Sexy," he comments on my outfit and heat rises in my cheeks. Compliments like that don't exactly make me not want to sleep with him. Especially when he's sitting there looking so damn sexy.

"You look sexy too," I reply.

"So," he changes the subject to my surprise and puts down his smartphone.

"What do you want to know?"

"Hm," I say, trying to figure out where to start. "Let's start with the scar."

Noah sighs and touches the spot where it is.

"Logan and I had a fight. He's five years older than us. He was eleven and I was six. Alex and I were teasing him and he picked up one of our toy cars and threw it at me. It hit me here," he taps the scarred tissue above his left eyebrow, "and I got this scar".

"Couldn't he have defended himself any other way?"

"Of course he could," he says, laughing. "But this was the most efficient from a seven-year-old's point of view. He always had to stand up to two little brothers. Alex and I always stuck together."

"Against Logan?" I guess, and Noah laughs.

"Against Logan, yeah," he agrees. "Alex and I were and are a unit."

"I see," I mutter. "So how did Alex manage to find a girl-friend - without you?"

"I wasn't allowed to sit next to him anymore and Daisy was put there," he answers with a laugh.

"Did you like her?" I ask.

"Daisy?"

I nod.

"Sure," he says. "I still like her. We're all the same age, and we still get together when we're in Nashville. We're friends."

"That's nice," I say. "That you're still connected."

"I think so too," he says, smiling at me. "It's our home, and sometimes it's good to get away from the stress of Boston."

"Why are you going to Nashville this time?" I want to know.

"It's our mother's birthday and it's the Fall Fair."

"The Fall Fair?" I ask curiously, because I've never heard of it.

"You really don't know anything about it, do you?" Noah replies amused.

"No," I say, biting my lip. "I'm from Boston and I've only lived in big cities. What do you do there?"

"During the day it's a market where local farmers sell their goods, there's food and drink. Of course, there are a lot of car-nies and live bands. We try to go every year. And the Fall Fair is always held around our mother's birthday."

"That's the official reason, of course," I tease him.

"Absolutely!" Noah laughs too. "Every year we get drunk on our mom's birthday because there's a big party at the Fall Fair the night before. Once Alex came straight from the fair to the birthday breakfast."

"Oh God!" I exclaim. "And what did your mom say?"

"She was mad, but she laughed it off," he says, shrugging his shoulders. "What else could she have done?"

"Right," I think, wondering if something like that has ever happened to me, but quickly deciding that it hasn't. My friends all come from families where such celebrations are avoided, and family birthdays are always a highly official social event, so you can't afford to do that.

Noah's stories sound fun. It must have been great to have such a liberated childhood.

"Okay, go on," I urge him. "What about your tattoo?" He holds out his wrist and I nod.

"'A' for Alex and 'L' for Logan," he explains. "And I like the crown."

"Very nice," I say, reaching out to trace the lines with my fingers. The tattoo is not new, it has run a bit, but it is still beautifully drawn and you can see how much it means to him. How much his brothers mean to him.

Noah looks at me and leans over. He reaches for my hand and plants a kiss on the inside of my wrist. Goose bumps form on my body, and I look at him with big eyes. Noah doesn't even think about leaving it at that one kiss, but continues to kiss his way up my forearm. Finally, he lifts his head and looks at me.

My heart pounds in my chest as he leans forward.

"What are you doing?" I want to know in a hushed voice.

"What does it look like?" he replies playfully. "I have to convince you that there are better things to do than chat."

"Like what?" I ask, moving toward him. Noah meets my gaze and overcomes the last few inches between us to place his lips on mine. He kisses me softly. His lips explore mine. Sighing, I surrender to him, placing my hand on the back of his neck and kissing him back. Our tongues greet each other. Noah pulls me astride his lap. My core touches his hardness and we both moan.

Noah's hands run down my back to my butt, which he gently squeezes and kneads. I know he's about to pull up my shirt to touch my bare skin. I moan at the mere thought of him touching me further. The desire to feel his lips all over my body grows. I rub my pelvis against his, feeling his hardness beneath me. I want to pull his hard dick out of his pants and just push my panties aside to give us both some relief. Spurred on by my own thoughts, I slide my hands down his chest to my stomach and the hem of his t-shirt. Without breaking the kiss and asking permission, I let them slide underneath. His steel-hard abs welcome me. Noah moans as I trace the ridges of his six-pack with my fingernails. His dick rubs against my intimacy, covered only by the delicate fabric of my underwear.

"Noah," I whisper, tugging at the hem of his shirt. "May I?"

"Yes," he whispers, helping me and throwing it on the floor next to us. I look at his muscular chest and run my fingers over it. He looks so good. Why not extend our friendship with this small but nice thing? Good sex never hurt anybody. Why shouldn't 'friends with benefits' work for us?

Noah pulls me closer and places his lips on mine. I kiss him back, put my hands on the back of his neck and slide my tongue into his mouth. We both moan as my center slides over his and now it's Noah who lifts the jersey and pulls it over my head. It lands on the floor next to his and he looks at me. My breasts are in a see-through bralette that gives a perfect view of my hard nipples. Noah's lips explore my neck. He sucks the thin skin over my pulse into his mouth and releases it. This is going to be a hickey for sure.

"I want you," he moans, pulling me closer. His kisses move over my shoulders to my breasts. His hands on my back keep circling the clasp of my bra. "Do you want me too?"

"Yes," I whisper, smiling at him.

Noah turns us over so I'm underneath him. He slides between my legs, and his lips find mine again. From there he works his way down my neck to my breasts. He gently licks my nipples with his tongue. The thin fabric of the bralette becomes damp from his saliva and sticks to my heated skin.

"Noah," I gasp, lifting my pelvis.

He laughs against my stomach, giving me goosebumps. Noah looks up at me and straightens up to place his lips on mine. He places his hands next to my head and lowers his pelvis against mine. He warms me even more with circular movements. It feels incredibly good.

My fingers make their way over his chest and stomach to the hem of his shorts again. I gently slide my hand inside and he moans against my mouth as my fingers touch his hot shaft.

"God!" he gasps, moving his pelvis back and forth.

I grab his penis and move my hand up and down. Again and again, I let it slide over his heated sex, right up to his glans.

"Cara!" His hand reaches for mine and stops me. I look at him with a grin. My hand is still gripping his dick and although he holds me tight, he gives me enough room to continue stroking it. Finally, he pulls my hand out of his pants and places it next to my body.

"Leave it," he whispers. "Please."

"Why?" I ask. "Do you usually get off fast?"

Noah's eyebrows shoot up, and I laugh in amusement. That's definitely a yes.

"You're driving me crazy," he whispers, kissing my neck, breasts and stomach again. When he reaches my panties, he spreads my legs wide and pushes his broad shoulders between them. The soft kisses on the inside of my thighs almost make me jump.

"Noah, please," I gasp as his hot breath hits my sensitive center.

"You're so perfect," he whispers before hooking his fingers into the waistband of my panties and pulling them down. I moan loudly as he presses his mouth to my center.

"Noah," I moan, lifting my pelvis to meet him. He separates my labia with his tongue and penetrates me with his finger. My moans light up the bedroom, and I come to him. The tip of his tongue circles my most sensitive spot again and again, making me claw my fingers into the blanket beneath me. My pelvis jerks up, but Noah pushes it down with ease.

"God, yes!" I scream as he adds a second finger. It doesn't take long for me to reach my first climax.

Incredible feelings of happiness rush through my body and I close my eyes contentedly. Noah pulls away from me and I only just notice that he takes off his shorts and boxers and pulls me against him by my knees. My eyes fall on his hard dick sticking out between our bodies. I look at it and my fingertips dance over his hip bones.

"You're so hot," I whisper to him.

Noah bends over me to open the drawer of his nightstand. He pulls out a condom. I smile at him and he smiles back. My heart races as he takes the condom out of the wrapper and slips it over his hard length. Excited, I bite my lip as he leans over me and positions his dick at my entrance, only to penetrate me the next moment.

"Noah," I gasp as he stretches me. My fingers dig into the hard muscles of his shoulders. He penetrates me inch by inch.

"Oh God!" It feels incredible to feel him inside me. My eyelids flutter slightly as he is completely inside me.

"Are you okay?" he asks and I nod.

I wrap my legs around his hips and my arms around his neck as he leans into me.

His lips find mine again, and he gives me a passionate kiss before moving inside me.

14

NOAH

Nashville, Tennessee, a few days later

I smile when I see Cara's surprised look. Her eyes widen with every mile we get closer to my parents' house. There are no mansions, pools, or gated neighborhoods here. There are cute row houses with yards and the occasional small store and gas station to complete the picture of a town just outside of Nashville.

It is certainly a culture shock for Cara - from the big cities of the East and West Coasts to a small town in Tennessee.

Although she is quick to point out that her parents come from normal backgrounds and that her dad made a lot of money playing football and her mom made a lot of money modeling, she has never lived that life. It was always normal for Cara to have millions of dollars at her disposal. She got everything she wanted and never lacked for anything. But she also often told me that material things could not replace the attention of her parents, especially her father. My parents, on the other hand, were present at every school party, every game, and every important event in our lives.

"Do you like it?" I ask, looking over at her.

Cara smiles.

"Yes, very much," she says, giggling. "I'm so excited to meet your family."

We met yesterday at her office and talked about a campaign I'm supposed to shoot next week. It's a perfume commercial. I told her on Sunday that I was going to Tennessee. So, yesterday, I spontaneously asked her if she wanted to come with me. Cara was surprised at first and didn't know what to say. But then she agreed. I realize that I may be reading a little too much into this trip. I like Cara, I like her a lot, and I'm happy that we're going to my parents' house together.

"Here we are!" I say, parking the rental car in the driveway of our house. My parents' cars are parked in the garage, and I look over at Cara with a smile. I told my mom I was bringing someone from Boston. She immediately wanted to know if it was a woman, and I said yes. What else was I supposed to do? She knows all of my friends and knows that they have other plans at the moment. As you might expect, she was beside herself.

I deflected all further questions about how I felt about Cara and whether she was my girlfriend, insisting that we were friends. My mom didn't believe a word of it.

"It looks beautiful," Cara says, smiling at me. The house must be tiny to her. The Corses' villa is huge. If not gigantic.

"That's it," I reply, turning off the engine. "Let's get out of the car."

Cara unbuckles her seatbelt and I do the same. We get out of the car, and I look at her with a smile. Before I can say anything else, the front door opens and my mom walks out.

"Noah!" she calls, walking down the three steps of the porch and toward me. "How nice to have you home."

"Hi, Mom," I say, giving her a hug. Smiling, I plant a kiss on her cheek. "Are you okay?"

"Everything's fine," she replies, looking past me to Cara. My eyes follow hers and I grin. Cara looks at us shyly.

"Mom," I clear my throat. "This is Cara. Cara, this is my

mother, Charlotte."

"Hello, Mrs. McCarter," Cara says with a smile and walks over to her. "Thank you so much for inviting me."

"You don't have to thank me," my mother replies immediately. "And please call me Charlotte."

Mom gives me a grinning look.

"Come in, come in. Logan and Alex are watching TV with your dad."

She looks at me again, then at Cara and turns to go into the house. Cara still looks a little nervous because of my mom's behavior as I walk up to her.

"Are you okay?" I ask, pulling her close. I keep catching myself seeking her closeness and wanting to have her with me. It feels too good to miss. Especially since we had sex - which was absolutely amazing. I'm not averse to doing it again, but I can't tell how Cara feels about it.

She looks up at me, and I wrap my arms around her. I put my hands behind her back and grin at her.

"I think so," she says. "And you?"

"Me too."

"I hope your mom isn't thinking the wrong thing?"

"Believe me," I sigh. "She believes what she wants to believe since I said I was bringing someone. No matter what we say. Don't worry about it."

"Someone or me?"

"You," I say, searching her eyes. I want to lean down and kiss Cara, but I can't. My parents and brothers are probably standing behind the curtains in the house like the cavalry, just waiting for us to kiss. Cara doesn't want a relationship, she's not ready.

"Maybe we should go inside," she says. "What do you think?"

"We should," I say, pulling away from her. I take two steps

back and grin at her.

"Come on, come on. I'll get our luggage later."

Cara nods and joins me. Smiling, she leads me to the house and we enter. I am immediately surrounded by the familiar surroundings of my childhood. We often offered to buy our parents a bigger and better house, but they always refused. They thought that just because their sons were earning millions, they didn't have to snap and give up their home.

"You can hang your jacket on the coat rack," I say, taking off mine. Cara complies and follows me into the living room.

As my mom had announced, Dad, Alex and Logan are sitting in front of the TV. My brothers are on the couch and Dad is in the massage chair he got for his birthday a few months ago. Cara looks around curiously. Our jerseys are hanging on the wall above the big TV. There are photos all over the place. Mom can't get enough of showing off her sons.

"Hello," I say, smiling at her. "Let me introduce you."

"Hello," Cara says shyly and my mother smiles at her. She clearly likes her. I can tell by the way she looks at her. She has the wildest fantasies in her head about Cara and me. She would probably prefer Cara to be my girlfriend, but she isn't.

"This is Cara," I introduce her. "Cara, this is my dad, Peter, and my big brother, Logan. You already know, Alex."

"Hello," she says again, raising her hand. "I'm glad to be here."

"We're glad you're here," Logan says, standing up to shake Cara's hand. "You definitely got the quieter twin."

Logan winks at me and I roll my eyes. Alex protests, of course, and gives Cara a kiss on the cheek as he passes.

"Hello, Cara," Dad says, smiling at her. "You'll have to excuse these three childish boys. They're still the same rascals from Tennessee."

"No problem," she says. "It's really great to be here. What

are you watching?"

She walks past me to the TV.

"A replay of Logan's game from last week," he answers. "Do you like football?"

I can't help but laugh softly. Alex joins in and hands me a beer.

"A little, sir." Cara looks at me and I wink at her. Alex and Logan sit back down on the couch.

"Come on," I say, pointing to the second TV chair.

Cara looks at me skeptically. I sit down and pull her onto my lap. She seems uncomfortable, but my brothers and dad don't notice us. Instead, they analyze the game.

"That wasn't a touchdown!" shouts Alex in disgust. "No way!"

"Of course it was," Logan counters. "The ball was over the line."

"It wasn't!"

Cara looks at me and I shrug.

"It's always like this here," I tell her. "Don't be surprised. Would you like a drink?"

"Not right now," she says, looking at the TV, which is now showing a charge by the opposing team. The defense of the Nashville Warriors is really bad. Logan buries his face in his hands.

"Let's watch Noah and Alex's game against Seattle," he suggests to avoid his own embarrassment.

"No!" Alex and I shout. The game was a disaster, and I don't need to see it again. Cara laughs and I give her an annoyed look.

"What?" she says with a grin. "Are you afraid they're going to tear you apart?"

She nods at my dad and Logan.

"No," I lie, even though I know they would.

"Good thing I record all your games," our dad says, changing the channel. I groan and lean back. Cara grins at me and looks at the TV. The game was a disaster.

"You can see right away that Noah is out of position," Logan analyzes, his mouth full again. "The Seattle defense knew right away."

I roll my eyes. I know that myself.

He doesn't have to tell me.

"Oh, come on," Cara says. "They came back in the last quarter, but then they were too stubborn." My dad rewinds to the scene she's talking about. "That's right!" Cara shouts. "You wanted to go up the middle and score the touchdown yourself. Toby is wide open in the end zone."

I roll my eyes and my brothers and dad giggle quietly.

"You could have easily thrown over Seattle's defense. Instead, you wanted to be the hero and let a rookie show you up."

Dad and Logan yell, Alex laughs, and I roll my eyes.

"Thanks, Cara," I say sarcastically. "We never would have thought of that."

"Please," she says, laughing and puts her hand on my neck. I jump for a moment because I wasn't expecting it. Her fingers caress my skin. Once again, a touch between us goes far beyond friendship.

"You really know your stuff," my dad praises her, smiling at Cara. "Football fan?"

"Kind of," she says with a grin and looks at me. "It runs in the family."

Her little white lie makes us all laugh and makes my dad look pretty stupid.

"Why are you laughing?" he asks, reaching for his beer. "It's great that she's interested in football."

"No, no," Cara says, waving him off. "My dad played football too."

I bite my lip to keep from laughing out loud. The way Cara says it is really too cute. Our dad is still on the fence and raises his eyebrows questioningly.

"Oh yeah?" he asks. "Where?"

"Boston and Atlanta," I answer and he nods.

"That sounds very good. Great teams. When was that? The Boston Foxes were very successful in the 1990s. They won a couple of Super Bowls."

"They did," Cara says. "My dad won the Super Bowl four times with the Foxes."

Dad's eyes get as big as plates, and he almost falls out of his chair.

"Four times?" he gasps. "Who's your dad, that's an extraordinary achievement."

Alex laughs again and Logan grins broadly. Dad looks at them questioningly and demands an answer from his sons.

"Michael Corse," Cara says quietly and there is silence.

Dad gasps for air and then laughs out loud.

"Good one, girl," he says. "Who is your father really?"

"Michael Corse," Cara says emphatically. It's the first time I've seen her upset because people don't believe her. "He's my dad."

"Michael Corse?" he asks again. "Quarterback legend, most voted MVP and..."

"Five-time Super Bowl winner Michael Corse is my father, yes," she says, "You don't believe me?"

"That's...wow." Dad's eyes fall on me. "And you didn't tell me?"

"It's not my job," I answer with a shrug. "Michael is Cara's father."

"Amazing," Dad says appreciatively. "He really is the greatest of all time."

"To me, he's my dad," Cara says, snuggling up against me. "It's weird that everyone thinks of him as a football superstar. He's just my dad."

"We believe you," my mom says, sitting on the edge of the chair next to my dad. "When Logan was the first of the three to go to the NFL, it was strange for us, too, that everyone saw our son as a star. When Noah and Alex followed, it got even stranger, but they'll always be our sons, up to no good."

"Not me!" shouts Alex, raising his arms and walking toward the kitchen. "I'm the boring sandwich boy."

"You're the worst!" Mom shouts, laughing and throwing a towel after him. "Get Cara something to drink."

"Yes, Mom!" he shouts ruefully and I have to laugh and pull Cara even closer to me. She smiles at me and I know she's comfortable and had no problem with my dad's questions.

★★★

Cara and I enter the basement of my parents' house and I lead her to one of the guest rooms. These used to be our rooms when we were kids. Today my parents use the empty rooms mainly for their hobbies and guests. Alex went out again and I bet he has a date. Logan went back to his apartment. It's only a half hour drive to Nashville.

"This is where you sleep," I say, pointing to the big bed, the dresser and the small nightstand.

"Okay," she replies, "your family is really nice and funny. I'm looking forward to tomorrow."

"Me too," I say. "I hope you'll like my friends too."

I walk over to Cara and stop right in front of her. She looks up at me, and I look back at her. I gently reach out with my right hand and brush a strand of hair behind her ear. She smiles and bites her lips, which looks extremely hot.

"Are you going to the bull riding?" she asks.

At dinner Logan and Alex told us about the annual bull riding at the Fall Fair. Cara thought it was awesome and now wants me to go.

"No," I reply, shaking my head. "No way."

"Why not?" she wants to know. "I'd cheer for you too."

"Oh, I'm sure you would," I answer, pulling her close. "The risk of me hurting myself with such nonsense is too great."

"Oh, right," she says and sighs, "too bad."

"You would have liked to see that, wouldn't you?" I hiss and lean over to her. "Would I have gotten a reward?"

"Maybe," she whispers, responding to my little game. "What do you have in mind?"

My stomach tickles and a thousand things I want to do to her go through my head. This teasing and flirting between us is great and shows me that I'm not fighting a losing battle.

These are the moments when we are just us. I'm the boy from Tennessee who has a huge crush on the girl in front of him, and she's the cute college student from Boston. Not the mega-rich daughter of a football legend.

"Hm..." I pretend to think, but I don't have to. "Maybe a kiss."

"A kiss?" Cara asks, raising her eyebrows. "That's pretty high stakes, don't you think?"

"No," I say. "Maybe you can give me a taste and I'll think about whether it's worth it." I'd probably be stupid enough to sit on this animal for a kiss from her. But the risk of injury is still too high. I can't risk it and I don't want to.

"It's okay, Mr. McCarter." Cara puts her hands on my neck and pulls me down to her. I bridge the last few inches between us and press my lips to hers. Cara immediately kisses me back and snuggles up against me.

My tongue brushes her lips and separates them. Cara opens

her mouth and allows my tongue to enter. We moan as our tongues touch and my hands find their way under her shirt.

Without comment, I push her onto the bed behind us.

15

CARA

Noah didn't exaggerate when he told me about the Fall Fair. There are many booths with food and drinks, carnival rides, and booths where you can buy all kinds of trinkets. What I find most impressive is the Ferris wheel, its bright colors are shining over the fairgrounds.

"Wow," I exclaim as Alex and I stroll through the market.

In front of me is a stage where a band is playing country songs.

"Do you like it?" asks Noah next to me.

"Absolutely," I answer. "You weren't exaggerating! It's amazing."

"I never do," he says with a wink. My thoughts take a new turn and get stuck on last night. The fact that we had sex again was absolutely not planned. We're just friends. But somehow, we're getting deeper and deeper into it. It feels way too good with him - everything. Noah is great and so is his family. His dad finally got over the shock that I was Michael Corse's daughter and had a casual conversation with me. He also didn't ask about Dad, which I have to give him credit for. Usually, people always want to talk about my dad.

"There are the others!" Alex calls to us, pointing to a group standing together at a bar.

Noah and I follow Alex.

He greets the men with a handshake and kisses the women on the cheek.

"Noah!" one of them shouts. "You're here!"

He has short brown hair, is much slimmer than Noah, and wears a blue T-shirt and blue jeans. He makes a nice impression.

"Hey!" Noah spreads his arms.

The two of them embrace, much closer than Alex. I stand at a distance behind Noah and smile. What else can I do? I don't know anyone here except for the McCarter twins.

"Let me introduce you." Noah turns to me and smiles. "This is Cara. A friend from Boston. Cara, this is Jamie, my best friend."

"Hello," I say and shake his hand. "It's a pleasure to meet you."

"The pleasure is all mine," he replies with a smile. "What would you like to drink?"

"We'll both have a beer, right?" Noah gives me a quizzical look and I nod. Beer is not one of my favorite drinks, but here it seems to be the drink of the masses.

We approach the bar together, and Noah introduces me to the rest of the clique. There's Ned, a friend from school, with his girlfriend Kelly and her friend Natasha. And Harry, another friend from school.

Noah introduces me to them and to my surprise they don't notice me or ask me any questions. It's nice to see Noah surrounded by his friends he's known since childhood.

"Alex, Noah!" a woman's voice calls out and I turn around. A beautiful blonde woman is walking towards us. She is tall and slender, her hair falling in soft waves over her shoulders.

"Daisy!" Alex circles the table and greets her exuberantly. Daisy? I look at Noah, who nods weakly as he greets her, too.

I stand still, not moving, waiting for her to finish with them. Daisy plants a kiss on Noah's cheek and I bite my lips to keep my mind on something else. For some reason I don't like her getting so close to Noah. She wraps her arms around him like she owns him. Isn't she Alex's ex-girlfriend?

I press my lips together, trying to suppress the uncomfortable feeling called jealousy. I don't want to be jealous because there's no reason to be. Noah and I are not a couple. I'm not in love with him. He's my friend, nothing more.

It seems to me that Daisy has a knack for causing trouble.

"Oh God, Days!" exclaims Noah, shaking his head. "I want you to meet somebody."

Noah turns and looks at me. I look back at him, and when he smiles at me, my heart skips a beat. His eyes say so much, but there's no way he's romantically or sexually interested in Daisy.

"This is Cara," he introduces me. "Cara, this is Daisy."

"Hey," she says, friendly, shaking my hand. "Nice to meet you. I didn't know you had a girlfriend."

"He didn't either," I clarify. "I'm just a good friend. Cara, nice to meet you."

"Oh!" Daisy looks at Noah and then back at me. "I didn't know, sorry. I'm glad you're here."

I have to say, she's really nice. Damn. Usually, my first impression isn't wrong. Daisy smiles at me again and turns to Harry and Alex. Noah takes a step towards me and puts his arm around my waist to pull me close.

"Are you jealous?" he whispers so quietly that only I can hear him.

"What?" I squeak, panic spreading through me.

"You don't have to be jealous," he says. "Not of Daisy."

"And what about other women?" I blurt out immediately. I guess I'm confirming his assumption that I'm jealous.

137

"Nope," he replies, planting a kiss on my temple. "Now come on."

Smiling, he takes my hand and pulls me back to the bar. No one comments, the group just continues their conversation. In Boston this would be a scandal. Or maybe Noah has women here all the time and they're used to it? Maybe he's the big player here and not Alex. That would also explain why he's never mentioned a girlfriend.

An uneasy feeling spreads through me and I put some distance between me and him. I don't want to be one of many, but I also don't want to be the one. He's a football player, and I don't want to be with a football player.

Jesus, it's all so complicated.

"Do you think her bag is real?" I jump when I hear a female voice to my left and turn my head. Two young women are standing next to us, watching me. I look directly at them, and they give me a challenging look back.

"I don't know," the brunette says. "Noah must have given it to her because she is spreading her legs."

I gasp indignantly. What kind of wicked women are they? I'm not going to let anyone give me a Chanel bag for sex.

"Lucky her," the blonde giggles. "I wouldn't say no to that either. To the bag and to Noah."

Stupid cows! They're just jealous.

"Don't let them tease you." I jump and turn around. A young woman with shoulder-length brown hair stands before me. Her curves make her stand out from the crowd of small-town women our age, but not in a bad way. She has great charisma and an incredibly pretty face framed by her long bob. "Oh, sorry. I'm Emily."

"I'm Cara," I say. "It's okay ... there are interesting people here."

She laughs and glances at the two women who just judged

my bag and, more importantly, my sex life.

"Welcome to Tennessee. Where are you from?"

"I'm from Boston," I say. "I'm here with Noah."

I point to him and Emily nods with a smile.

"Cool," she says, "how do you two know each other?"

"I'm his agent," I reply. "And you?"

"I'm not his agent," she replies, giggling, and I join in. "Alex used to date my sister. We went to high school together."

I look at Emily in surprise, then at Alex and Daisy, who have caught up with us, and then back at Emily. This can't be right, can it? Emily and Daisy are sisters? They look nothing alike and when I say nothing at all, I mean it. Daisy is blonde and slim and Emily is dark-haired and curvy.

"Daisy is your..." I look back and forth between them again. "Sister?"

"Yes!" Emily laughs. "Hard to believe, isn't it?"

"Kind of," I say, looking back at Daisy. She's still standing next to Alex, talking to him. I bet they'll end up in bed tonight, the way they're flirting with each other. "I can't believe it."

"Not just you." Emily shrugs, as if that's the usual answer. "No one would think we were sisters."

"Emily, hey," Noah says, walking past me to give her a hug. "Where did you come from?"

"I was saying goodbye to Anna," she says, smiling. "You have a lovely friend!" Emily winks at me and I blush. Noah laughs and puts his arm around me.

"Nice of you to say that," he says with a grin. "Would you like a drink?"

"I'll take a Cosmopolitan."

"They have cocktails?" I ask, looking down at my beer. "Why didn't you tell me?"

Noah rolls his eyes and looks at Emily reproachfully.

"Thanks," he says. "I thought I could fool her with the

cheap beer."

"You're impossible. Typical McCarter," Emily grumbles. "She should be worth more to you than a two-dollar beer."

"The cocktail's seven," Noah says, and Emily shakes her head.

"You make ten million dollars a year, Noah McCarter. I think you can buy this lovely lady a cocktail for seven dollars."

I like Emily more and more.

"That's okay," I say, opening my purse and pulling out twenty dollars. "I'll go to the bar and get a caipirinha. What would you like?"

"Another Cosmopolitan," she says, and I nod.

"Daisy?"

She looks at me in surprise.

"Yes?" she asks, looking irritated that I'm talking to her. "Hey, Em."

"Hey, Days," she says. "You want a drink?"

"Sure," she says, "Are you getting cocktails?"

"Yeah," she says, "what would you like?"

"I'll have a Bloody Mary, thanks," she says, and I nod.

"Here." I push the beer into Noah's hand. "We'll get something decent to drink."

He laughs and pulls me towards him. Surprised, I bounce against his muscular chest. He leans down and plants a kiss on my ear.

"Have fun with Emily," he says. "You'll love her."

I smile at him again and walk with Emily to the bar.

She's really super nice, and we have a good time. Like me, she's twenty-two and works as a physiotherapist in the city. She has known Alex and Noah since they were kids and, of course, because Alex and her sister used to be a couple. I would be interested to know if she ever had a crush on one of the twins. But that's too private, we haven't known each other

140

long enough for that.

Emily and I have conquered the dance floor. Laughing, I sip my fourth or fifth cocktail. I paid for all of them, which Emily didn't like very much, but I didn't make her pay. To be honest, I have no idea how much she earns, but it will be less per month than the cost of my bag. I can't reconcile it with my conscience that she's paying for these far too expensive cocktails for me.

"Shall we go back to our table?" I call over the loud music. She gives me a thumbs up. We start walking together. Our group has thinned out a bit. Only Noah, Alex, Jamie, Emily and I are left. Logan disappeared with a blonde, and Daisy hasn't been seen since. She's nice, no question, but I never really connected with her. She was always too close to Noah. I put my drink down on the table and look at Noah with a smile. He's just as drunk and I have no idea how we're going to get home.

A new song comes on and I sway back and forth.

"Do you want to dance?" Alex asks Emily. Her cheeks turn pink and she shyly pulls in her lower lip with her incisors. Oh dear, that answers the question I asked earlier.

Emily has a crush on Alex.

"Yeah, okay," she says, "why not?"

He grabs her hand and pulls her to the dance floor. I smile, because Alex is spinning Emily around.

Noah wraps his arms around my shoulders and pulls me into his chest. Smiling, I put my hands on his forearms and lean against him. Alex is just twirling Emily around the dance floor, but they're having a lot of fun together. I have to admit that the two of them are really cute together. Too bad that Emily doesn't seem to be Alex's type. The women he dates in Boston - and Daisy - are the complete opposite of her.

"They're cute together, aren't they?" I ask, looking at Noah.

He laughs.

"Alex and Em?"

"Yes," I say. "I think they're cute. They make a good couple."

"Alex and Em?" he repeats.

"Yes!" I shout. "Why do you keep asking me that?"

"Emily's like a little sister to us," Noah says. "Alex dated her sister and regularly ends up in Daisy's bed when he's in Nashville. Him and Emily? No way."

I look back at the dance floor and sigh. Alex is pulling Emily towards him, making their dance more sensual.

"Too bad," I say, turning to him. "I think she's very nice and I think she'd be good for Alex."

"How about that," Noah says, pulling me closer to him. "We stop worrying about Alex and Emily and take care of ourselves?"

"Hm," I confirm, wrapping my arms around his neck. "Sounds like a plan."

16

CARA

The next day Noah, Alex and I meet up again with Jamie, Emily, Daisy and Harry. This time not at the Fall Fair, but in a bar in town. The interior is cozy and has a rustic charm. According to Noah, once a week there is a free stage where you can sing or perform. I've learned so much in the last two days in Nashville. The people here are so incredibly nice, and I liked Emily right away. Even though we seem to come from completely different worlds, we really get along.

"Hi," the waitress says, and I realize that she is one of the women who gossiped about my Chanel bag yesterday. Great, that's all I need.

"What can I get you?" she asks, looking around.

"Four beers," Noah orders. "And what would you like?"

"A Cosmopolitan and a Caipirinha," Emily also orders.

"Of course," says the waitress. "On the rocks?"

Grinning, she turns to Noah.

"Yes, please," he says, and she turns and stomps away. I watch her for a moment and turn to Noah. He puts his hand on my thigh, without comment, but hidden from the others under the table. The spot he touches tingles pleasantly.

"I'll tell you," Harry says. "That was the sickest car I've ever driven."

He has my attention.

"Which one?" I ask and he looks at me like I'm kidding. As if it can't be a matter of interest for a woman.

"Sorry, but I don't think that's your area of expertise, Cara." Well, I'll say!

Well, unfortunately, it's exactly my area, because I love cars. Noah smiles and I raise my eyebrows.

"Is that what you think?" I ask. "Why?"

"You don't look like you know anything about cars and horsepower," he answers casually. "Right guys?" Asking for his buddies' approval, he looks around. "No offense, okay?" he adds.

"Why don't you tell me what kind of car it is and then you can think about whether I have a clue or not," I reply sourly.

Harry blushes and his friends, Daisy and Emily, look at him challengingly.

"I work in a garage and recently drove a Ferrari there."

Now we are getting closer.

"Model?" I want to know and Noah can barely hold back his laughter.

"It was an SF90 Stradale," he replies, as if I'm finally out of the conversation. But I'm not, and the fun is just beginning.

"Sounds good," I reply. "The engine runs fine if you give it a good kick. But don't put too much stock in it."

"Wha... what?" he stutters. "Have you ever driven a car like this before?"

Alex and Noah laugh out loud and Jamie looks back and forth between us, irritated.

"I drive it every day. It's good, no question, but you should drive a Lamborghini Aventador sometime. It's really fun."

"Come on, Cara," he says. "The joke's over now, yeah? Let it go."

"I don't know what your problem is and why you think I'm

not capable of having a serious conversation with you about cars. But if you don't know what's good and what's not, maybe you should stick with a Ford or a Dodge."

"Okay, fine!" Oh dear ... I've dented his ego. "Then tell me why you can compare Ferrari and Lamborghini?"

"Because I own them," I blurt out. "And before you ask, a Porsche 911."

"Wow!" Daisy exclaims. "Where did you get all that money?"

Now everyone is looking at me and I regret opening my mouth. Of course, they want to know how a twenty-two-year-old can afford these cars.

"None of your business," Emily defends me.

"It's okay," I say, giving Emily credit for stepping into the breach for me. "My parents are very wealthy," I reply evasively. "Is that enough of an answer?"

Daisy blushes and averts her eyes. And I'm glad the waitress comes over with our drinks and sets them down in front of us.

"Thank you," I say politely and she nods. She probably doesn't like me very much and still thinks I'm sleeping with Noah for a Chanel bag.

"Okay, guys!" The bar gets awfully loud, and we turn our heads towards the stage. A man about our age is standing there with a microphone in his hand. "Welcome to tonight's free stage. Are y'all enjoying your evening?" There's clapping and cheering all around me. The guy introduces the first act, and we fall back into our conversations.

"You should perform, Noah," Daisy says, putting her hand on his upper arm. I look at him questioningly and then at her. What does she mean? Does he have some talent I don't know about?

"No," he says, waving her off. "Not today."

"Come on," Jamie encourages him. "You really have what

it takes."

"No, and I don't have a guitar."

"I think that's the least of your problems," Emily giggles next to me, but I don't hear her. I look at Noah and he rolls his eyes. Then I look at Alex and Jamie who are grinning.

"Noah can sing incredibly well," Emily finally tells me.

"I can't," he says, giving Emily a reproachful look.

"You can," she argues. "You almost had a record deal when you were sixteen."

"What?" I squeal. "Is that true?"

"She's exaggerating," he mumbles. "I was in a musical at school because I needed another class. Apparently, I was okay..."

"Uh-huh." My eyebrows shoot up. "There's a world of difference between doing okay in a school musical and getting a record deal."

"I ..."

"And apparently you can play guitar too. So ... what's that all about?"

"Yeah, well," he grumbles. "I can sing. Happy?"

I look at him and smile.

"I'd love to hear it," I whisper and squeeze his hand. "Please, Noah."

He squeezes his eyes shut and sighs after a few moments. He pushes back his chair noisily. The others clap when he raises his hands.

"Hey, Fred!" Noah calls out. "You got a guitar for me?"

"Noah, dude! I got every guitar in the world for you!" Fred yells back and disappears backstage.

Noah gives me a meaningful look that goes right through me and then heads for the stage. I turn around in my chair so I can see him clearly. He climbs on stage and the guests in the bar clap again. Fred hands him a guitar and places a stool for him to sit on. I watch him with fascination. I would never have expected him to be able to sing. This man is full of surprises.

Noah takes a seat on the stool and bends his right leg to rest the guitar on his thigh, wrapping the strap around his body. He looks incredibly sexy. And looking around, I'm not the only one who thinks so. Daisy is hanging on his lips, and he hasn't even made a sound yet. Emily is smiling too. The other young women in the bar are pining for Noah, too.

"Hi," he says, putting the microphone in front of his mouth. "Why do I always end up on this stage?" A collective laugh goes through the bar. "I'm just going to start. If you like it, you know that your donations are for Fred's bar, to which I'll add a zero as usual."

The bar goes quiet, as if everyone is waiting for him to start playing. And he does. Noah's fingers glide over the guitar strings, and I form my mouth into a silent "Wow" - even though he hasn't sung a note yet.

When he sings the first few lines of a song I don't know, I can't stop marveling.

Noah has a beautiful voice.

"He sings amazingly," I whisper to Emily and she nods immediately.

"Unbelievable, isn't it?" she asks. "And you always have to make him do it."

Noah's eyes are closed and even I can tell he feels every single note. The chorus completely blows me away because he opens his eyes and looks at me at that moment.

He is singing a country song from the early nineties that I don't know, but I find it very beautiful. His voice completely envelops me and I hardly notice anything but Noah's soft tones and the sounds of the guitar.

I'm speechless. It's absolutely amazing. I can't believe he can sing. And so well. If he wasn't a quarterback, he'd be the perfect country singer.

Everyone in the bar stands up and claps when he finishes. Noah grins sheepishly and puts down his guitar. He seems uncomfortable with the applause, and I can hardly believe it. My heart is beating faster for him. His voice has absolutely enchanted me and made me even more enthusiastic about this man than I already am. This trip to Nashville makes our relationship even more blurry.

"Thank you," he says. "We can get back to our evening."

He hands the guitar to Fred, jumps off the stage and comes back to our table. The others have sat down, but I'm still standing, looking at him with big eyes.

"You can ... sing," I say and he laughs when he reaches me.

"A little," he says shyly. "It's no big deal."

"No big deal?" I ask. "You sang incredibly. Just amazing and..."

"Cara," he stops me. "It's no big deal."

Noah sits down in his chair, and I do the same. Noah takes my hand and smiles at me. I slip my fingers between his and grin. The song was incredibly beautiful. The others think so too. They shower Noah with praise - especially Daisy, but then she snuggles up to Alex again. That woman is a mystery to me. She always hits on Noah and then goes over to Alex. Strange ...

"When are you going back?" Emily asks in our direction. I'm about to answer when Alex and Daisy stand up.

"We're off, guys," he says, raising his hand.

"Bye," Daisy says, waving. I wave back briefly and turn back to Emily. But her expression has completely changed. Her eyes are fixed and her incisors are digging into her lower lip. There's no sign of the happy young woman she was a few minutes ago. I look back at Alex and Daisy, who are leaving the bar hand in hand, and then back at Emily.

"I'll be right back," she says suddenly and disappears.

I open my mouth to shout something after her when Noah catches my attention.

"Are we going too?" he wants to know and smiles at me.

"I... I don't know," I mumble and look for Emily again, but she's gone. "What about Emily?"

"I don't know." Noah shrugs. Typical man. "I think she thinks our siblings' behavior sucks as much as I do."

I don't think that's the reason, but I'm not going to tell Noah. She didn't seem angry, she seemed hurt. After all, Alex swept her across the dance floor yesterday and who knows what happened between them? And today he's screwing her sister? Holy shit. These small-town dynamics can be weird. But who am I to judge?

"I want to say goodbye to her, okay?"

Noah nods and smiles at me. "I'll go ahead and pay for us."

It doesn't take me long to find Emily in the bathroom.

"Hey," I say. "Are you okay?"

She stands at the sink and runs water over her wrists.

"Sure," she replies, turning off the faucet and grabbing wipes from the dispenser.

"Really?" I ask, grabbing her forearm. "I saw you and Alex yesterday and today..."

"There was nothing going on between me and Alex," she replies hastily. "He likes my sister."

Emily looks at me for a moment and then storms out of the bathroom. I'm speechless for a few seconds before I follow her. Something is wrong, but that's not my business. I leave the bathroom as well, and Noah is standing in front of me. He has our jackets in his hands.

"Shall we?" he asks and I nod.

"Yes," I say. "Where's Emily?"

"She's back with the others," he says, holding out his hand. I take it and follow him out of the bar.

★★★

Noah and I walk onto the porch of his parents' house and I sit down on the swing. Noah sits next to me and pulls me close. Smiling, I snuggle up to him and wrap my arm around his torso.

"Why didn't you ever tell me you were such a good singer?" I ask, looking up at him.

"I didn't think it was important," he says. "And it's really no big deal."

"You sing so well," I reply. "Don't say that."

"Cara," he sighs. "It's no big deal. Yes, I can sing, but that's all."

"You're so modest," I chuckle and look at him.

"Like you are when it comes to cars?" he asks me the counter question. "You took the wind out of Harry's sails."

"Oh!" I bite my lip. "I didn't mean to, but I like cars and..."

"You don't have to explain," he replies and puts his hand on my cheek. I snuggle into it and close my eyes. The days with him in Nashville have been wonderful, and our friendship is moving more and more in a direction that can no longer be called friendship. At least that's what I think. Noah and I are slipping more and more into something we can no longer control. He looks down at me and gently presses his lips to mine. I kiss him back and put my hand on the back of his neck, pulling him closer.

"The shock did Harry a lot of good. I don't think he always realizes that these aren't luxury cars for Alex and me either, but normal vehicles."

"That's right," I mumble. "Your friends are nice."

"You like them?"

"Sure," I say. "Especially Emily."

"I noticed," he replies with a smile. "You get along really well."

I want to go back to the Alex and Daisy thing, but I don't want to put Emily in a stupid situation. I don't think anyone has figured out why it really bothers her that Alex and Daisy are having sex. "Alex and Daisy are having sex, aren't they?" I blurt out. Heat rises in my cheeks and I look away. The worst thing I could have said, I say. It's none of my business if they're having sex. I don't want Noah to put the pieces together and think I asked for this because of Emily. Personally, I couldn't care less if they have sex.

"I'm sure they are," he says with a shrug. "It's nothing new."

"But why?" I ask.

"Well, why do we have sex?" he asks me the counter question and I look at him. I think for a moment and then laugh.

"Well," I say, sitting astride Noah's lap. Grinning, he puts his hands on my hips. "Because it's fun and pretty good."

"I'm sure it's the same with Alex and Daisy," he replies. "In the end, they have to figure it out for themselves. I like Daisy, but she's annoying. She gets Alex's hopes up unnecessarily."

Noah presses his lips to mine, ending the conversation. It's better for all of us. Finally, I blurt out my suspicion that Emily is secretly in love with Alex.

17

NOAH

Boston, one month later

Cara throws back the covers and gets out of my bed. I watch her and a grin appears on my lips. Her long brown hair falls down her back, and I check out her hot body.

She walks through my bedroom and collects her clothes, which she miraculously lost last night.

It has been a month since we were in Nashville. In that time, we have grown closer and closer. Hardly a day goes by without us being in touch. Even though I have to travel through the States once a week, we usually see each other the next day or the same evening. Cara is still reluctant to use the word relationship, but I think we have one.

She's always at my house, so my brother is already joking about whether it's still our apartment or Cara's and mine. I have feelings for her. Real feelings that go way beyond the initial crush and sexual interest. It's starting to bother me that I can't tell her and show her this openly. But I'm afraid that if I do, she'll end things between us. Cara is fighting her own demons on this subject, and I don't know how to overcome them. I know she feels comfortable with me. But as soon as I try to encourage her to have a serious relationship, she stops me and runs away. Maybe I'm imagining too much about our time together.

But it's just not true that her heart doesn't get just as out of sync when we kiss, or that her skin doesn't tingle just as treacherously and get covered in goosebumps when we're close. I mean, can you fake goosebumps? Orgasms, yes, but goose bumps?

I shake my head. I shouldn't be so paranoid. These thoughts are absurd.

But Cara doesn't want a relationship with a football player because she doesn't want to live her mother's life. Even if she has feelings for me, she won't show them openly.

"Come back to bed," I ask, looking at the clock on the television. "It's only half past six."

"I have to go to work," she replies with a grin, pulling up her panties. "And get something to wear first."

"What about that dress from yesterday?" I ask as she grabs her bra. "Can't you put it back on and we'll sleep for another hour? At least."

"No," she says, "I have a series of important meetings today. I can't show up in yesterday's dress."

I groan in annoyance and pull myself out of bed. Cara looks at me with a grin and I know exactly what she's thinking but not saying for many reasons.

"I'm going to take a shower," I decide.

"See," she says, grabbing her dress. "You have to work too."

"See you tonight?" I ask, slipping into my boxers.

The NFL Sports Awards are tonight. I am nominated - for Quarterback of the Year - and I want Cara to go with me.

"Noah," she groans, "how many times do I have to tell you?"

We've been having this discussion for over a week and can't find a common denominator. Cara refuses to go with me, even though she will be there. I even offered to do it officially as my agent, but she wanted it even less. If she had her way, it would be best if we weren't seen in public at all. Not that I mind that she prefers to spend our time together having sex, but I - damn it, I want more. I don't want to be the guy she spreads her gorgeous legs for. Well... not just because that feels damn perfect every time.

I want to be all that and more for her, just like she is for me. I want her to introduce me to her parents and finally admit that we're in a relationship.

"How many times are you going to tell me you're not coming?" I reply, annoyed. "What's your problem?"

"What's that supposed to look like?" Cara shakes her head and closes her dress.

"Damn it!" I walk up to her and push her hands away. She wants to walk away and resist my help, but I won't let her.

"Hold still!" I growl. "Why won't you come with me?"

"I can't," she sighs and I do the same. I kiss her neck gently. "I really can't and besides, you can go with Alex."

"I don't want to go with Alex," I reply. "Please, baby."

I push her hair aside and kiss her neck more intensely. I suck on her sensitive skin with my lips, hoping to give her a hickey. Cara sighs softly and I grin to myself. I've already won so far. I gallantly turn her around and push her in front of me.

"Hands on the bed," I tell her.

"Noah!" she calls, half giggling, half warning, rubbing her sweet ass against my crotch. "I have to work."

"Come on," I whisper, continuing to kiss her neck as my hands find their way under her dress to her panties. I pull them down with ease. I caress her wet pussy greedily.

Cara moans as I push two fingers inside her and place my thumb on her pulsating clit.

"Bend over," I whisper and this time she complies. I quickly pull my penis out of my boxers and pull her dress over her butt. She stretches it out towards me, and I don't miss the opportunity to give her a good smack on her beautiful ass.

"Noah!" she gasps, wiggling her hips back and forth.

We've been making love without a condom for a few days now. We're both clean and she's on the pill.

I pull my finger out of her pussy with a smacking sound.

"Noah," she moans again. "Please."

"You're so ready for me, baby," I whisper, sliding my glans between her folds. Cara moans as I slowly insert myself into her. "So fucking wet."

Centimeter by centimeter I penetrate her until her tightness surrounds me completely. I place my hands on her hips and thrust into her. Her body jerks forward and she moans loudly. Her slender fingers bury themselves in the blanket while my hands leave beautiful marks on her hips.

"Faster," she encourages me.

I increase the pace of my thrusts and feel her tighten around me. This is what I love about sex with her. When she's on the edge and gets tighter and tighter.

I fuck her hard and fast until we're both close to coming. I find it hard to prolong it, but I don't want her to come right away.

My right hand finds its way between her legs, and I caress her clit. Cara screams and her muscles contract. She orgasms violently and I hold her until I'm ready too. With a loud moan, I come inside her and enjoy it for a few seconds. I make her mine.

Fuck, that sounds so wrong. She's not mine, that's just wishful thinking. But after a number like that, I can't help it.

"That was amazing," she whispers as I pull out of her, my cum running down her thighs.

"It was," I reply. "Shower?"

I help her to her feet and pull her close to me. I unbutton her dress and she takes it off.

"I don't have a choice, do I?" she says after looking down at herself. Grinning, I take her in my arms and kiss her thoroughly.

★★★

"Morning," Cara greets my twin and looks at him with a grin. Alex returns her look and sips his coffee.

"Morning," he greets us. "Did you have a good orgasm?"

Cara immediately blushes and I give Alex a scathing look. It's so typical. He loves to embarrass Cara and once again he does it masterfully.

"Coffee?" I draw attention to myself. After sex in bed and in the shower, I'm awake now.

"Maybe I won't have coffee after all," Cara sighs. "I really have to go."

She points to the front door with her thumb.

"I'll see you tonight for sure. Bye Alex."

"Bye," my brother replies, smiling at her. "Will you dance with me?"

"After seeing your dancing skills with Emily?" Cara laughs, raising her eyebrows. "No way."

"Oh, come on," he says, wiggling his eyebrows. "I can also dance very romantically and lead well."

Annoyed, I slap him on the back of the head.

"Don't do that," I growl. "You can push any woman in this country across the dance floor for all I care, preferably your ex and her little sister, but not Cara."

"Don't be jealous, little brother," he says arrogantly. "I can show your sweetie the ropes."

I roll my eyes, because it's another reference to the sex noises he's heard. Alex is my best friend, and, of course, he knows more about my sex life than Cara would like. Even

157

though I don't explicitly tell him what we do, he knows my preferences in bed well enough to know how it went this morning.

He also knows about my feelings for her and would never seriously flirt with her.

We both know what's good for us. With Cara, we both agree that she's good for me. Which is more than I can say for Alex and the Cluster sisters. He keeps falling in love with Daisy and he should keep his hands off Emily. She's way too good for him. I see Em one day in a fancy little house like our parents have, with a man who has a solid job and not her sister's playboy ex-boyfriend.

When I think of Daisy and me... yikes! That's totally against the bro code. I'm sure it's the same between sisters.

"Leave her alone, Alex," I say, putting my coffee down next to him. "I'll walk you to the door," I turn to Cara.

She nods and reaches for her bag that she left on the dining room table last night.

"See you tonight, Alex," she says goodbye again. "Have fun at practice."

"Thanks," he says and I follow her to the front door.

"Don't let him bother you," I say, grinning at her. Cara returns my grin.

"Neither do you," she says. "He's doing it out of pure provocation."

"Hm," I grumble and go to kiss her, but she turns away. "What is it?"

"Not here," she says, "Alex can see us."

"Alex can hear us making love," I counter angrily, raising my eyebrows. "Why shouldn't he see this?"

"I don't want him to," Cara clarifies and I press my lips together to avoid starting the next argument.

"We're not together, Noah. There's no reason for us to kiss

outside of the bedroom or sex. Especially in front of your brother."

"You don't say," I growl. I don't like that she's always emphasizing that we're not together. "See you tonight?"

"Sure," she says, "I'll see you tonight."

Cara smiles at me again, turns on her heel and disappears from the apartment. I run my hands through my hair, and groan in annoyance as the door slams shut. Frustrated, I go back to Alex, who smiles and hands me my coffee.

"Thank you."

"I'm sorry," he says. "I didn't mean to..."

"You didn't," I say, turning the cup in my hand. "For her, it's just sex."

"And not for you?" Alex asks and I shake my head. He basically knows, but I understand that he needs to hear it from my mouth.

"No, it was never like that," I sigh. "I like her, I really do, but she doesn't want to. She's sticking to her decision not to have a relationship with a football player."

"Fuck," Alex mumbles and I nod. "And there's nothing you can do about it?"

"No," I say, taking a sip of my coffee. "I can't force her to be with me."

"Yes, you can," Alex says and I roll my eyes. "I'm sorry, but she also has to realize that it's good between you. You're happy."

"You don't have to tell me that," I reply brusquely. "Tell Cara."

"You really want me to talk to her?" he offers.

I widen my eyes. Is he serious? There's no way he's going to talk to Cara and tell her how I feel about her. Firstly, I can do it on my own and secondly, she'll just take it the wrong way.

"No," I reply. "You shouldn't."

"Okay," he says. "Then go ahead and wallow in your heartache."

"I'm not wallowing..." I press my lips together. "Leave me alone, Alex."

"Yeah, what now?" he asks. "Do you want my advice or not?"

"No," I say firmly. "I don't want it."

Then I grab my coffee and go upstairs to pack my things for practice.

I love Alex, but he really doesn't need to give me relationship advice. I'm not heartbroken. At least I don't think I am. Heartache is something else.

18

CARA

I get out of the limo behind my parents and want to put my hand over my face. The NFL Sports Awards are a huge event and I hate being in the spotlight. These events are just meaningless. I'm aware that I'm pretty much the only person for miles around who sees it that way.

The man at the car gives me a friendly smile and I grab my dress and follow my parents. The dress is floor length and has a halter-neck. The neckline is cut wide, and my breasts are held in place with adhesive pads. The back is completely bare - from the neck to the tailbone. My father wears a simple black suit and my mother a dark blue dress that is much tighter than mine. It comes up to her knees and has an off-the-shoulder style. She looks beautiful as always and beams at my dad. It's strange that I want don't want my life to look like hers, and yet at the same time I long for it. My parents have been married for twenty-five years, together for twenty-seven, and they are still so happy. I want to have a relationship like that and find the right man. But so far, he's not in sight. Although that's not quite true. He is in sight, but I don't want him. He's a football player by profession and that goes against all my principles. There is absolutely nothing official between Noah and me and yet I miss him like hell when he's not around. How would it be if we got together? It'll just get worse, won't it? I know he wants more. Noah expects a relationship from me, and maybe this event today would have been a clear statement. Not only to the public, but also to him.

My parents walk down the red carpet, and I stand behind them at a distance. My dad is being honored today for his life's work, and that's the only reason I'm here. I'm so proud of him for what he's accomplished. He's the greatest player of all time, and they're honoring that tonight. My mom waves me over, and they take me into their midst.

Dad looks at me with a smile and gratitude in his eyes. He knows I'm only doing this for him and that deep down I hate it.

"Thank you," he whispers. I smile at the cameras and do my best. The reaction tells me that I did the right thing by being here for him today.

As soon as the pictures are taken, I sneak off toward the entrance. My mom follows me while my dad does a few more interviews.

"Ms. Corse, Mrs. Corse," a man says to us at the entrance. "May I escort you to your seats?"

"Sure," my mom says, joining me. "It means a lot to your dad that you're here today."

"Why do you say that?" I sigh. "You're making me feel guilty for not enjoying it so much."

"That's good," she says, "then you'll realize the implications."

I roll my eyes, which makes her laugh.

"Is Noah here?" she asks and I roll my eyes again.

"What do you think, Mom?"

Of course, she hasn't missed the fact that we're seeing each other. I'm sure she can guess that we don't just watch TV when we hang out. After all, she and my dad were young and dated once. Something I don't want to think about because they are my parents and Noah and I are not dating. We are friends with benefits.

"I think he's here. Didn't he want to come here with you?"

"Maybe," I dodge her and sit down in our assigned seats.

"Maybe?" My mom doesn't let up and I roll my eyes. "What do you mean?"

"I told him I was coming with you," I answer.

"Why?" she continues.

"Why not, Mom?" I reply, annoyed. "Noah isn't my boyfriend, and if we came here together, it would be weird, wouldn't it?"

"But you spend so much time together," she says, "and to be honest, your dad and I thought you'd finally introduce us."

"What does that mean?"

"He's your boyfriend, isn't he?"

"No," I say indignantly and am glad when my dad catches up with us and sits down next to my mom.

"Let's drop the subject," I decide.

My parents want to meet Noah as my boyfriend. Where will we get to if I introduce them to every guy I go to bed with? No, that's not going to happen. Noah and I are not a couple and we never will be.

I look at my phone and see that I have unread messages from Marina and Noah.

Noah: Are you there yet?
Cara: Yes, and you?
Noah: Just got here.

I close the chat and check Marina's texts.

Marina: Have fun tonight! Are you with Noah?

I roll my eyes. Of course, Marina knows Noah is here. But why does she think we're here together? I sigh. It could be because she's the president of the Noah McCarter and Cara Catherine Corse fan club. Marina thinks I should finally give in and start a relationship with him. After all, I have nothing to lose. She's not entirely wrong. So far, what I have with Noah has been good for me and I like being with him. But I don't want to. I have my principles and I'm not going to break them for Noah McCarter. I puff out my cheeks and answer Marina.

> *Cara: I'm here with my parents.*
> *Marina: Yes, and? Your dad is going to win an award anyway.*
> *Cara: We are not discussing that anymore.*
> *Marina: But we are still discussing it, because one has nothing to do with the other.*

I groan in annoyance and my mom gives me a questioning look. I wave her off and go back to talking to Marina when someone taps me on the shoulder. I turn to see Alex grinning at me. Noah is standing next to him, looking much more tense than his brother. He scrutinizes me. His eyes glide over my body, but the corners of his mouth don't turn up.

Doesn't he like me? Heat rises in my cheeks. If there's one man I want to please here, it's him.

"Hey!" I get up from my seat and let Alex kiss me on both cheeks. This draws my parents' attention to the McCarter twins.

"Hello, Mrs. Corse," Alex says, greeting them formally as well.

"Hello," she says, smiling. "Hello, Noah."

"Hello, Mrs. Corse," he says, smiling at my mother. "You look great."

I smile and my mom thanks him. Noah and Alex shake my dad's hand and chat with him.

I'm irritated that Noah doesn't greet me, but I don't question it. I prefer to look at him. He's shaved, which makes his features look a little too soft. I prefer it when he has a little beard. The tailored dark blue suit suits him perfectly, and the red handkerchief is the same color as my dress.

"Are you sitting behind us?" I ask and Alex nods.

"Right behind you," he says, winking at me. "I can sneak gum in your hair."

"And I can slap you in front of everyone when you do that," I reply and my mom laughs. "I wasn't joking."

"Of course not," Alex says amused and sits down. I look back at Noah, whose attention is completely focused on my dad. When my mom joins the conversation and one of the NFL's most important officials appears next to them, I sit down again.

"Hey!" I jump to see Noah's grinning face in front of me. He's resting his forearms on the back of the chair next to me.

"Hey," I whisper. "Why do I always notice that scar?"

I lift my hand and place my fingers on it. He grins and shrugs.

"I don't know. Maybe because you find it sexy."

"Maybe," I mumble. "You look great."

"Thanks," he says. "I'd like to tell you you look great too, but I'm not sure I should."

Okay, I wasn't expecting that. Don't lose your cool now. It's quite possible that he doesn't like my outfit. Under no circumstances should I let him see how upset I am. Noah has never refused me a compliment before. I bravely smile away the obvious rejection, even though it affects me. It's not nice when the man you desire and think is the most attractive man on the planet doesn't tell you you look great.

"Cara?" asks Noah. "Are you okay?"

"Sure," I lie. "Everything's fine."

"Good," he says and pulls away.

I expect him to pull away from me completely, but he doesn't. Noah leans back in and plants a kiss on my bare shoulder. Goose bumps immediately spread across my skin and butterflies flutter in my stomach. Where did they come from?

"You look beautiful," he breathes. "The dress is gorgeous."

Noah pulls away from me and I turn to face him. He sits down in his seat with a grin and pulls out his phone. When he looks at the screen, I turn away as it vibrates in my clutch. I pull out my phone and see that he sent me a message.

Noah: Can I take it off later?

I giggle.

Cara: Why?

Noah: Then you can undress me too? Deal?

Cara: But it takes me longer because you're wearing twice as much. Do you think that's fair?

Noah: Do you think it's fair that I have a hard-on? That dress should be banned!

Cara: And I thought you said I was beautiful. I'll think about it!

I send the message and turn my head to look at him again. Noah looks back at me and winks at me. Then he turns to Alex and speaks to his brother. I look back at the stage and put my phone down. Gradually, the room fills with all kinds of people. Current players, former players, club owners, officials and coaches. Of course, a few top celebrities are also in attendance. I try to ignore Noah behind me and concentrate on the award ceremony.

★★★

The after-party takes place in an old factory building near the harbor. I look around the room, keeping an eye out for Noah, when I'm stopped.

"Brick!" I call, beaming, and let myself be pulled into his arms. "How good to see you."

We went to college together and had a few classes together. He got drafted by Miami this year.

"The pleasure is all mine," he says. "Tell me ... what are you doing now? Where are you working? Who are you dating?" His questions inevitably make me laugh. Brick has had a girlfriend since college, and she's here, too, but he can't quite stop flirting with me.

"I've moved back in with my parents for now, but I'm officially looking for a place," I answer. "Besides, I work for Corse Sports Management."

"Of course," he replies, winking at me. Brick had an athletic scholarship and that was his only chance to go to college. His parents are from a poor neighborhood in Detroit. We hit it off and when he heard who my dad was, he was speechless. He said he had never met anyone as rich and yet as polite as me. He could introduce me as I am to his mother and she would never know I was an upper-class girl.

"And who are you dating?" He wiggles his eyebrows and grins at me.

"She's dating me!" An arm wraps around my waist and Brick's eyes go wide. I turn and look up at Noah's face. His lips are pressed together in a thin line and he looks at Brick with hostility.

"Noah, nice to meet you," he introduces himself unnecessarily. Brick knows exactly who is standing in front of him.

"I'm Brick," he replies in a friendly manner. "Nice to meet you."

"Nice to meet you, too," Noah says, slowly relaxing. His fingers brush over my hip as he slips the hand he just extended to Brick into the pocket of his pants. I don't need to say that I'm pissed at him. This has gone way too far. What is he thinking? Brick could be a potential client of mine, not an old friend. How does it look for my friend, who is not my boyfriend at all, to mark his territory in such a pathetic way?

"See you around," Brick says, raising his hand with a smile. "Nice to meet you, Noah."

I doubt he was really happy about it. Otherwise, he wouldn't turn around so quickly, would he? Brick moves away from us and I pull away from Noah.

I turn to him angrily and look at him.

"Tell me, are you completely nuts?" I bark at him. Noah opens his mouth to say something, but I don't let him get a word in. "What was that all about? Why are you pretending to be my boyfriend?"

I shake my head in disbelief.

"I'm not going out with you and I don't intend to. You know that. So would you please stop pretending that we're together?" I continue to vent my anger.

"Come on!" he growls, grabbing my wrist. I have trouble keeping up with him in my long dress and high heels. Noah drags me down the hall behind him. Past my parents, Alex and Toby and a few other familiar faces and, unfortunately, members of the press. We're at a big event where everyone's just waiting for a scandal to break, and we, of all people, are going to provide it? Noah knows how much I hate all of this. And now he's making sure I'm the absolute center of attention.

"Noah!" I call. "What are you doing?"

Ignoring me, he just keeps walking until we pass the security guard at the entrance and come to a stop in front of the building.

Furious, I yank his hand away and place it on my hip.

"Tell me, are you okay?" I yell at him, pointing at the entrance. "What was that about?"

"What... that..." He shakes his head. "You better tell me what it is about this Dick..."

"His name is Brick!"

"I don't care what the guy's name is," he yells. "What was that about, Cara? Can't you see how he adores you?"

I want to throw a snarky 'Like you?' at him, but I don't dare.

"He has a girlfriend. And even if he did," I answer, trying to calm myself down. This is an absolutely fucked-up situation, and we're in public, at the NFL Sports Awards after-party. We can't be here arguing and sorting out our relationship status. "You're making a scene."

"A scene?" he asks. "For making it clear to all those slobbering bastards, including my brother, that you're taken?"

"I am not taken!"

"Yes, you are!" he shouts. "By me."

I can't help but laugh, because he's probably going crazy right now. I'd probably know if I'd agreed to a relationship with Noah McCarter.

"You're out of your mind!" I yell, shaking my head. "We're not together and we never will be."

I start to walk past him, but Noah grabs my hand again and stops me.

"Cara, please," he whispers. "Why can't you just admit that you're in love with me too?"

His question hits me with full force. Like a punch I didn't

see coming, knocking me to the ground. My heart begins to race and the spot on my wrist where he touches me threatens to go up in flames. Noah's eyes go right through me. He seems so vulnerable right now that I want to throw myself into his arms to comfort him. But I can't, and even less so after his performance earlier. If we're unlucky, tomorrow the whole country will know we're screwing. Including my parents. Even if I have feelings for him, he's still a football player.

"Because it's not like that," I say. "I'm not in love with you. We're friends who occasionally sleep together. Nothing more."

19

CARA

Last night was an absolute nightmare. After Noah and I had a fight in the street, I took a cab home. I definitely didn't want to party anymore.

I didn't want things to escalate. I kept trying to reach Noah, but he wasn't answering his cell phone.

"Can you explain this to me?" my dad shouts.

His head glowing red, he slaps a Boston daily newspaper in front of my face. It takes me a moment to react and glance at the front page. My blood freezes in my veins and I swallow hard when I see the headline.

"This!" my father continues, tapping the front page with his index finger. "Explain it to me!"

I pick up the paper with shaking hands. It's the Boston Sports Radar, the most important sports paper in the city. And on the front page is a picture of me, my parents and Noah!

I was expecting to see a picture of my parents and me. After all, my dad was being honored for his life's work. It's a photo from the red carpet, but where does Noah fit in? I quickly scan the headline: 'Noah McCarter: Quarterback Ends Affair with Corse's Daughter!'

I quickly open the paper and look at the article. The pictures are all from last night. One with my parents and the rest with Noah and Alex - and the press is accusing me of having an affair with both McCarter twins. They're crazy!

"What is all this about?" my father asks, crossing his arms over his chest. "How can I read something like that about my daughter?"

My parents are not at all used to such lapses on my part, and I understand that they are angry. Mom comes up behind him, but unlike him, she doesn't look angry, she looks worried.

"This is... this... this was and I..." I shake my head. "I can't explain it. I'm sorry."

"Cara Catherine Corse," he says sternly. "It says he wants you, that you want him..."

My dad doesn't want to talk about my sex life in the paper, and that's a good thing. I don't want that kind of stuff coming out of his mouth.

"Noah and I had an affair," I try to explain. "And I ended it yesterday. That's all."

"And that's what all the fuss is about?" he asks.

"He started it!" I shout like a petulant child. "He dragged me out of the building, paraded me in front of everyone, and started this fight in the street - not me."

"Don't blame Noah," my father replies. "You did your part too. Everyone's talking about the story. What are you doing, Cara?"

"Leave her alone, Michael," my mom interjects, giving him a dirty look. "She made a mistake. So what?"

"A mistake?" He gasps for air. "There are videos circulating on the Internet of our daughter giving the Boston Foxes quarterback..."

"None of this would have happened if he wasn't a quarterback!" I yell at my dad. "If you weren't a quarterback, I wouldn't be stuck in this shitty life!"

Suddenly my mood shifts from vindication to sadness and

frustration. Tears stream down my cheeks, and I vehemently wipe them away. I don't even know why I'm crying. Because of my dad, because of the job, because of Noah or because I'm just stupid? I don't know.

"Honey!" My mom comes over and strokes my back. "What's wrong with you and what does this have to do with your dad?"

"I'd like to know that too," he barks at me. "Didn't I make everything possible for you and your mother and ...."

"Did you go to one of my performances at school?" I ask. "No, because you were playing football! Did you go to my high school graduation? No. You were never there, Dad. That sport was always more important than me, than us, and I swore I didn't want to live like that. Not like Mom."

"Cara!" My mother exhales. "You think I was unhappy?"

"I know," I reply, standing up. "I need to work this out with Noah."

"I wasn't unhappy," my mother says. "Lonely sometimes, maybe, but never unhappy. I always had my greatest happiness with me."

I open my mouth to speak when my mother sighs.

"Cara, you were all I needed. Your father and I, we never got bored in our relationship and always had something to talk about. I missed him, of course, I did, but I had you. I was never lonely. Before you were born, I often traveled with him. It was a great life, the best, and I have never regretted it."

"Really?" I breathe and she shakes her head.

"No," she says, "and it tears my heart apart that you think that and that's why you're throwing this wonderful man away." Her eyebrows shoot up. "Is he that bad in bed?"

"Mom!" I scream, my face turning crimson.

My father groans in frustration.

"Dana!" he grumbles. "I don't want to know, and Cara,

173

honey..."

He runs his fingers through his hair and I can clearly see that he is struggling to find the right words and composure.

"I'm sorry," he says, and I look at him in surprise. After that performance, I didn't expect him to react like that. "Why didn't you say anything?"

"Football has always been the most important thing to you and it's the most important thing to Noah and ..."

"Nothing is more important to me than you and your mom. You're my daughter, my only child. And if you're throwing away the man of your dreams because of that, then I've failed as a father in every way."

"You didn't fail, Dad."

"But?"

"I can't imagine a life like that," I say honestly. "Not for me and not for my children."

My mother smiles at me.

"Sometimes you have to take risks to be happy. When we got together, your dad was already a star and on the road all the time. And you know what life is like with a football player, honey."

I look at my mother and sigh.

"But I... I messed up," I whisper, wiping away my tears. I say nothing more and leave the kitchen and my parents. I don't want to talk to them anymore.

When I try to reach Noah again, he doesn't answer the phone, of course. He also ignores my messages. I can understand that he's mad at me, but I have to talk to him. The whole thing is a disaster. My parents have threatened to sue anyone who spreads the video of our fight and the article. I think that intimidated them, but it doesn't change the fact that I need to work this out with Noah. The conversation with my parents, while confusing, has given me food for thought.

It's enough that I'm in love with him. Because that's what has always kept my mom by my dad's side. She loves him. That's why she's put up with all the hardships that life has thrown at her. It's the same with me. When I imagine a life without Noah because I can't get off my ass and panic about my childhood, I shudder. Noah and I have taken so many steps towards a relationship. We've been together all the time, getting to know each other's families.

The elevator doors open and I step out. With each step I take closer to the front door, I get more nervous. My hands are sweating and I try to ignore the uncontrollable pounding of my heart. So far, Noah's apartment has been a happy place for me. We've had some great times there. We laughed a lot and loved each other. It was always fun with Alex, too. Although I know that Noah isn't always happy with how freely Alex talks to me. But he doesn't have to worry about that. Because I would always choose Noah. Alex is funny and we have a lot of fun together, but I could never talk to him the way I talk to Noah. I think the right woman for the other McCarter twin is still out there somewhere. I just hope she's not in Nashville and named after a flower. Wait a minute. Why am I worrying about Daisy and Alex when I can't get anything together myself? Noah just dumped me last night.

I take another deep breath and press the doorbell. I regret it immediately and wonder what I'm doing here. Noah is going to kick me out, and for good reason. I've completely messed things up between us and caused a scandal like no other. Although... he's not completely innocent, is he? He confronted me and dragged me out of the building.

The door swings open and Alex looks at me in surprise.

"Cara?" he asks, his eyes wide.

"Hi," I whisper, feeling anything but comfortable in my own skin. "Is... I mean, is... can I... come in?"

"Sure," he says, stepping aside. I pass Alex and enter the apartment. "Where's Noah?"

"Not here," he answers.

I narrow my eyes and decide to stay calm. Alex is my only chance to find out where Noah is. I shouldn't be surprised that he's angry with me. Noah is his twin brother, and I've hurt him badly.

"And where is he?" I ask in a trembling voice.

"Out for a run," he says. "And I mean that seriously." A small smile plays on his lips. "A lot going on this morning."

"Uh, yeah," I say. "My dad took care of it."

Alex raises an eyebrow and I bite my lip. I probably shouldn't have said that. I shiver slightly, even though it's warm in the apartment, and I feel extremely uncomfortable in my skin. "So... how... how long has he been gone?"

"I don't know," Alex says. "Probably a while. Do you want something to drink?"

"You're offering me something?" I ask, surprised, and he nods. Alex puts two glasses on the kitchen counter and grabs a bottle of water from the refrigerator.

"Why not?" he asks. "I like you, Cara."

"Oh!"

Alex laughs and closes the bottle while I greedily reach for the glass to wet my mouth.

"Are you so surprised that I like you?" he asks. "I have to admit it hurts me."

"No," I say. "It's not that."

I set the glass down in front of me and bite my bottom lip nervously.

"Noah is your brother and I... I messed up..."

"You broke his heart," Alex says what I don't want to hear. I bow my head in shame. "And yes, that hurts me too. He's my brother, Cara. You can't treat him like your horny little toy because you want to get fucked."

"I never did," I hiss and look at him. "Don't ever say that again."

"You didn't, but that's how he feels," Alex adds. "Listen... I shouldn't be having this conversation with you, but Noah is unbearable. Really obnoxious, and I can't put up with that for weeks and months. So, I suggest that you ask him to forgive you."

"That easy?" I ask skeptically and he laughs.

"Of course not," Alex says. "He won't forgive you."

My shoulders slump sadly. My little glimmer of hope that it might not be so hard after all is extinguished.

"Then why are we talking?" I ask. "What do I do if he doesn't forgive me?"

"You have to apologize and ask him to forgive you," he advises me. "And it's hard to believe I'm saying this, but you're probably the best thing that's happened to us two idiots in the last few months."

I can't help but laugh.

"I heard what you said to Noah - about Daisy."

I bite my lips and lower my eyes. I did mean it, but it wasn't meant for his ears. Alex is a grown man and he knows what he's doing.

"And it's true. Daisy is taking advantage of me."

"Do you still love her?"

"Daisy?" Alex laughs. "No. I like her and I have fond memories of my time with her, but I don't love her anymore. We're friends with benefits."

"Friends with benefits?" I raise my eyebrows. "I don't know. I should go."

"Why?" he asks.

"I don't want to wait hours for him." Alex nods and I push my glass across the bar to him. "Thanks for the water and the conversation." I smile at him.

"Gladly," he says and nods. I slide off the barstool and turn to go to the front door as it opens. Noah walks in, kicking off his running shoes.

"I'm back," he says tiredly. You can see the strain of the last few hours on his face. "The run was really good, thanks, and..."

When he sees me, he stops immediately. His previously tired but gentle gaze hardens and makes my blood run cold.

"Get out!" I am completely unable to follow his words. "Go on, get out!"

"Noah, I..." I stammer, searching for the right words, but unfortunately, I can't find them. "Let's talk?"

"No," he says, grabbing me roughly by the arm. "I'm done with you."

"You're hurting me," I try to stall, but he rolls his eyes and drags me to the door behind him.

"Noah!" Alex interrupts. "Listen to her?"

I smile gratefully at him, but unfortunately it only seems to make Noah angrier.

"No need," he grumbles at his brother. "It would be nice if you stay out of my hookups in the future, like I've been doing with you and Daisy for years."

HOOKUPS?

He didn't say that did he? Angrily, I tear myself away from him.

"What did you just call me?" I hiss. "a hookup?"

"Yeah," he replies matter-of-factly. "That's all it ever was. Now get out of here."

I hear Alex say something else, but Noah doesn't answer his brother. Instead, he drags me to the front door, opens it, and pushes me into the hallway. I look at him with my eyes wide open.

178

"Noah," I whisper. "Please. Let's talk."

There is no trace of his usually gentle nature on his face. On the contrary, his expression becomes more and more rigid and angry.

"Fuck you, Cara!" he spits out. "I'm done with you, your games, and our relationship." Then he slams the door in my face with a bang and yells at his brother.

I stand there for a few more minutes, my lower lip trembling, and finally I burst into tears because I have lost the man I love.

20

CARA

Three weeks later, Noah continues to ignore me. He dodges my calls, my messages go unanswered, and he has suspended all of our business meetings until further notice. He can't even talk to me professionally. I don't understand him. If we talk, we can make things right, can't we?

I would like to apologize to him and ask him for a second chance. Then we can try being together and have an official relationship, I don't care, but I want him back.

On top of that, he got hurt the day before yesterday in the game against Nashville and didn't come back after halftime. A defensive player from the Nashville Warriors, Logan's team, knocked him down and hit his right arm. His throwing arm. It didn't look good from the start, but Noah wanted to keep playing. In the end, he didn't come back and I have no idea how he is. If he is badly injured or just a little bit. I don't know anything and it's driving me crazy. Alex doesn't answer me either. My messages are delivered to him, but he doesn't write back. I'm sure Noah gave his brother a good talking to and forbid him to contact me.

I walk into a Starbucks in downtown Boston and am on my way to the counter when I see Alex. He's sitting in the back of with a coffee. I think about walking up to him and talking to him, but I reassess the situation.

"What can I get you?" the barista asks, smiling at me.

"A macchiato." I look at Alex again and take the money out of my pocket.

"Four dollars," she says and I hand it to her.

"Thank you."

I walk to the counter and don't let Alex out of my sight. He's my only chance to get to Noah and find out what's wrong with him. I need to know how badly he's hurt and where he is. I pick up my drink and walk over to Alex.

Heart pounding, I stop in front of his table and take a deep breath before speaking to him.

"Hi," I say softly and he lifts his eyes. Alex looks surprised and immediately puts his phone down.

"Hi," he says, looking at me. "Are you okay?"

"Not really," I mumble, pointing to the empty chair across from him. "May I?"

Alex is hesitant, I can see that. But I also know that we've known each other long enough and that he likes me enough to offer me a seat.

"Sure," he finally says and I smile and sit down next to him.

"Thanks," I mumble, clutching my coffee to go cup tightly.

"How are you doing?" His question sounds sincere and I swallow.

"Not good," I admit to him. "I miss Noah."

"Hm," Alex says, scratching his coffee cup with his nails. "He's not feeling well either."

"Because of the injury?" I ask. "What's wrong with him?"

"It's his shoulder," Alex says and sighs, "at least three weeks off."

"Shit!" I blurt out. "How is he doing with that? Has he had physical therapy and does he need surgery?"

My questions are so stupid and not useful at all, but I don't

182

want to lose the conversation before it has really started.

"How should he be, Cara?" Alex shakes his head in disbelief. Ashamed, I bite my lip and look down at my cup. "Sorry" he rows back. "Noah is in Nashville getting his shoulder fixed."

"He's in Nashville?" I look at him. "How long?"

"I think two or three weeks," Alex says. "But I don't know ... he ... he's ... weird."

"Weird how?"

"He won't admit it, but he misses you, too." My heart speeds up at his words. "But he'll hardly be able to bring himself to talk to you again."

"I can tell," I murmur. "He is ignoring me...he rejects my calls, my messages, even our business appointments."

"I know," Alex replies, leaning back in his chair. "He can't be persuaded to reach out to you either. I'm sorry, Cara. I've really tried everything, but he just shuts down."

"I don't understand him," I say. "I realized my mistake, but now he has to listen to me."

Alex nods and sighs.

"I know," he says again. "I'm sorry."

Talking to Alex doesn't help either. He can't or won't tell me anything more. No one will be able to make Noah talk to me and forgive me.

"Are you leaving already?" he asks when I get up.

"I have to work," I answer evasively. "See you around."

Alex's expression is pained and I sigh. Slowly, I reach out and stroke his upper arm.

"Thank you, Alex," I say. "Really, thank you, but it's no use."

"I'll keep trying," he says, smiling at me. I believe him, but have little hope. Then I turn and walk out of the Starbucks.

★★★

Late in the afternoon, I'm not getting out of my Porsche in Boston to go to dinner with Marina, but out of a taxi in Noah's hometown, because I don't remember where his parents live.

"Thank you," I say to the friendly and very helpful cab driver, giving him a hundred dollars. "That's way too much, miss."

"No, no," I say with a smile. "You've helped me so much." And he really did. I tried to describe to him the exact neighborhood of Noah's parents' house, but the man couldn't help me either. I wish I'd remembered the address and written it down.

The taxi driver offered to drive me around the streets, but that didn't help either. Now he's dropped me off on the main street, and I've decided to eat at a diner and ask around. It's a small town, Noah kept reminding me that when I visited. Someone will be able to tell me where the parents of the famous McCarter brothers live.

"Then I wish you good luck, miss," he says, smiling at me. "The man would be a fool not to forgive you."

I smile shyly.

"Thank you," I whisper. "And I hope he forgives me."

He nods at me again and gets back into his cab. I reach for my bag and realize he dropped me off in front of a small diner. I go in and look around. The place is decorated in typical American style. The walls are covered with merchandise from the local sports teams and the local high school teams. There is also a photo of the McCarter brothers, how surprising. I find a table and sit down. Sighing, I sit back and run my fingers through my hair. I desperately need a game plan.

"Hi!" A young man smiles at me. "What can I get you?"

"A Diet Coke," I say and he nods.

"Would you like a menu?"

"Sure," I reply and he turns and disappears behind the

counter again. I take my cell phone out of my purse and see that I have a couple of messages from Marina.

Marina: Did you get there okay?
Marina: Cara?
Marina: Please contact me!!!
Marina: Are you okay?
Marina: Did you find Noah yet?

I grin because she's really cute when she's worried. Marina offered to come with me to Nashville, but in the end, she didn't want to sit on the plane unnecessarily because of the pregnancy. A super hysterical pregnant friend wouldn't help either. 99.9999% of the time she won't be able to find the right words to tell Noah.

Cara: Arrived safely!

"Your Diet Coke," the waiter says, setting it down in front of me. "And the menu."

"Thank you," I say, smiling at him.

"Is there anything else I can get you?"

"Yeah ... maybe," I mumble. "You know the McCarter twins?"

He blinks once and blinks again before laughing out loud.

"Who doesn't know Noah and Alex?"

"Right," I groan. "Who doesn't know them. And... do you know where they live?"

"Yes," he says and I can already see myself at the destination of my dreams. "So, where?"

He wedges his tray between his stomach and his hands and licks his lips. He looks at me with a grin.

"If I had a dollar for every woman who came into the diner asking for Mr. and Mrs. McCarter's address, I'd be a rich man." I roll my eyes. "Sorry, honey, but it's an unwritten rule around here that we don't give out the McCarters' address."

Somehow I respect his decision, but it frustrates me immensely. If the waiter is so secretive, what about the rest of them? I bite my lip and consider offering him a hundred dollars for the information, but that seems wrong.

"Okay," I sigh. "Too bad."

He nods at me and disappears. When he's gone, I grab the menu and open it. I go through each dish meticulously. But the only thing on my mind is Noah and how to find him.

"Cara?" My head jerks up. "What are you doing here?"

Emily is standing in front of me, eyebrows knitted together, looking at me. She's wearing white pants with chunky side pockets, the kind construction workers wear. Over them is a washed-out light gray polo shirt with a physiotherapy practice printed on it and a white long sleeve underneath. Such a beautiful woman and such an ugly outfit.

"Hi," I say in surprise. "Oh God ... I'm so happy to see you. What are you doing here?"

Emily giggles and sits down in the chair across from me, brown paper bag in hand.

"I'm getting my lunch, and you?"

"I'm desperately trying to find out where the McCarters live," I summarize. "From the looks of it, everyone here is very secretive."

"Yes, we remain stubbornly silent."

"Hm," I grumble. "Yeah, I've noticed."

"So," she says, unpacking her food. "What are you doing here if you want the McCarter's address?"

"I'm looking for Noah," I say. "He's here."

"He is," Emily confirms. "I'm working on his shoulder."

"You're working on his shoulder?" I ask. "Why are you telling me this now and ... and where is your office? When can I meet him there?"

Emily swallows the big bite of her sandwich before answering.

"Sorry," she says, "I'm really hungry."

"I see that," I chuckle. "How is Noah? What's wrong with him?"

"He dislocated his shoulder," she answers. "Nothing dramatic, but still three weeks out - at least."

"That's what Alex was hinting at," I say.

"Were you at the stadium?"

"No," she says, wiping the corners of her mouth with a napkin. "Daisy told me."

"Of course she did," I scoff, and Emily raises her eyebrows. Maybe I shouldn't forget that they're sisters and Emily doesn't take too kindly to me making fun of her sister. "Sorry."

"It's okay," Emily mumbles. "This thing between her and Alex is ... well ... complicated."

Of course, that's one way of putting it. Although I think she meant to say something else. Emily likes Alex, more than that, and I bet she doesn't like Daisy bragging about having sex with him at all.

"Back to you and Noah," she changes the subject. "Does this have anything to do with the newspaper article?"

"Kind of," I say. "Noah and I had completely different views on our relationship - or our being together, as I prefer to call it - and it escalated that night. In the worst possible place, and everyone saw it. He's been avoiding me like the plague ever since."

"Are you surprised?" she asks and I swallow.

Anxiously, I reach for my Diet Coke and take a sip.

"You really hurt him and even a blind man could see that you had a crush on each other. Why did you do that?" she scolds me.

"Because of his job," I confess. "I don't want to live like my mother and raise my children the way she did with me. It would all happen again with Noah by my side."

"I see," Emily says, leaning back. "I'm sure you know that Daisy broke up with Alex because she didn't want to either, right?" I nod. "To leave town and move further away than Nashville. She's too proud to admit it, but she regrets her decision and I think she still loves Alex."

I almost let an 'What about you?' slip out, but I manage to stifle it.

"And what does this have to do with me?" I ask.

"You're too proud to jump over your shadow, too," she explains. "You're afraid of what this job will bring. Moving and little time together. But if you love Noah and he loves you ... why are you being so stupid?"

"I'm stupid, not him," I clarify. "Noah wanted us from the beginning."

"And do you think he won't miss you and your children just as much?" she asks and I bite my lips. "I don't have a father who was gone every two weeks, and I didn't grow up in the spotlight. Ultimately, I'm judging the situation from the outside, but if you love each other, you'll make it. How long will Noah play? Ten or fifteen years at the most."

"It depends on how healthy he stays and..." Emily rolls her eyes. "That's not what you mean, is it?"

"No," she replies, "I mean that you shouldn't use ten or fifteen years as a standard for the twenty or forty years you have left."

"To be honest, I've never seen it that way," I say quietly. "I always saw my childhood and my mother. But you're right. My parents are happy and enjoying their retirement because they have enough money to have a nice life. They travel a lot."

"You see," Emily instructs me. "My partner and I will probably have to work until we're in our mid-sixties, or maybe longer if we don't have enough money." I refrain from saying that she wouldn't have to if she were at Alex's side. "While Noah and you get to enjoy life."

"You're not making me feel better," I mutter. "Not at all."

"Probably," Emily replies with a grin and stands up. She quickly packs her things. "I'll take you to my place for now. Come on."

I look at her irritated and get up from my chair.

Emily puts money on the table for my Diet Coke and smiles. "Come on, Cara."

"And what about Noah?" I ask again.

"I'll take care of it," she says, winking at me.

21

CARA

An uneasy feeling runs through me as I get out of an Uber after Emily that evening and we walk towards the bar we went to last time. It's not a good idea to spend the evening with Emily and her friends. Noah still doesn't know I'm in Nashville. I hope I don't run into him. But Emily wouldn't do that to me.

As I enter the bar, a wave of memories washes over me. Noah singing, holding my hand, and me falling a little more in love with him.

"Are you coming?" Emily asks when I don't move forward. "The others are waiting for us."

"I don't know," I say, looking at her. "It's not a good idea to face Noah like this for the first time."

"Cara!" Emily rolls her eyes. "It's not a solution for you to mope around while Noah continues to ignore you. That idiot should pull the stick out of his ass and forgive you."

To avoid looking like a complete idiot, I told Emily that I had written to him again and that he was still ignoring me. But the truth is, I don't dare write him any more messages.

"Come on!" She grabs my hand and pulls me behind her.

We walk through the crowded bar until I spot Jamie, Noah's best friend, at one of the tables.

"Emily." I stop and she turns to me. "What's Jamie doing here and - fuck!"

Noah is sitting in the chair next to him. He is laughing, in a good mood, greeting everyone.

"And Noah? You said we were meeting your friends."

"Actually, I said we would meet with the others. With Anna, among others."

"Among others?" I snort. "Clearly."

I look at her defiantly and wonder how this is going to look. Noah must think I'm using Emily to get to him.

"Come with me now," she says. "You're really unbearable."

Emily grabs my hand again and pulls me behind her.

Annoyed, I groan and follow her. After all, I can't remember where Emily lives and I can't get back to my stuff.

"Hey," Emily says to the group. "I brought someone."

She points at me with a smile, but I barely notice. All my attention is on Noah. He has his cell phone in his hand and is looking at the screen.

"Cara," Jamie moans and Noah's head jerks up. "How nice to see you."

"What are you doing here?" Noah interrupts his best friend before he can ask more questions. I say nothing and look at Emily. She has to help me. After all, she dragged me here.

"She's visiting me," Emily says with a shrug and Noah raises his eyebrows. "A little country air never hurt anybody, did it?"

Noah snorts and shakes his head dismissively.

"I should go," I whisper, biting my lip.

"You should," he adds. "Right now!"

"Nonsense," Emily says, pulling out a chair and pushing me into it. "What would you like to drink?"

I'm not sure how to react, but I'm not going to let Noah put me off so easily. If he gets away with this now and can continue to ignore me, he might do it forever.

"A caipirinha, please," I murmur and she nods with a smile. "I'll be right back."

Emily turns on her heel, leaving me alone at the table with the others. I know them all, that's not the problem. The problem is sitting across from me and he's fucking angry.

"And you're visiting Emily?" Jamie asks without smiling at me. I look at him unsure. I'm sure he's not asking out of pure interest, but rather as a provocation.

"Yeah," I answer, looking at Noah. He avoids my gaze and instead starts talking to the blonde next to him. My attention is on her now. She has shoulder-length hair, a slim figure and looks very nice.

"Here you go," Harry says with a grin.

He kisses the blonde next to Noah, and a wave of relief runs through my body. It's not his new girl.

"Here!" Emily puts our drinks on the table and sits down beside me. "Cheers!"

"I'm late!" Daisy calls, waving excitedly to the group. "Hey, guys! Move over, Jamie."

Jamie gives her an irritated look and Anna rolls her eyes. But then he does what she wants.

"Hey," she purrs, stroking Noah's arm. "Sorry I'm late."

He gives her a quick look and nods.

"No problem," he replies. "Do you want something to drink?"

"Some water would be great. After all, I have to drive."

Daisy winks at him and my jaw drops. She's screwing Alex, even though a blind man can see that her little sister is in love with him, and now that Alex is in Boston, she's hitting on Noah. Unbelievable.

And he seems to jump on it. He immediately gets up and gets her a drink of water.

"What was that?" asks Emily. "And where do you have to go?"

"Home," Daisy replies. "Hi, Cara. I didn't know you were here, too. Things have been a little crazy the last few weeks."

I gasp and start to say something, but Emily cuts me off.

"Don't do that, Days," she snaps at her big sister. "Cara didn't do anything to you."

"Can't she speak for herself?"

"Can't you leave her alone?" I put a hand on Emily's forearm and look at her.

"It's okay," I say. "And you: how many do you need it? Last week Alex, today Noah?"

Now Daisy is the one of us who takes a deep breath. I'm ready for her next low blow, but to my surprise she remains silent.

"What are you talking about?" she turns to Jamie, who unfortunately answers immediately.

Noah comes back and sets a glass of water down for Daisy. He got himself a beer, which probably means that they are actually going home together.

"Thank you," Daisy says, stroking his forearm.

I purse my lips and look at Noah. He looks back at me and sips his beer.

"Hey, Cara!" Harry smiles at me. "You said you know your way around fast cars, right?"

"Yes," I reply. "I do."

"Cool," he replies. "Have you ever driven a Bugatti Chiron?"

I shake my head and smile at him.

"Unfortunately not," I say. "I'd love to. It's definitely on my list."

Noah's eyes flicker to me for a split second and I give him a smile, but he immediately looks away.

"Where do you usually drive the cars?" asks Harry.

"On the road?" I answer questioningly. "They're mine."

"Sure," he counters. "They're yours. It was funny about the Ferrari, but..."

"My God, you're so stupid," Daisy groans. "Her father is Michael Corse, NFL legend of the Boston Foxes. She's going to inherit Corse Sports Management and her parents' personal fortune of at least fifty million dollars. Of course she can afford a Ferrari."

My head spins around and I stare at her angrily. Daisy gets on my nerves so much. She should mind her own business and not get confused about which of the McCarter twins is screwing her.

"What's your problem?" I hiss.

"My problem?" she repeats. "That you act like you're this sweet, sweet girl who wants to experience life in the country, when in fact you're as far removed from life here as Harry is from those cars he keeps talking about."

Daisy and I have an eye duel that neither of us wants to lose.

"Stop it, Daisy!" hisses Emily. "You don't even know her."

"And you know her?" she shoots back. "You've always been naive, Em." She points at me. "Her T-shirt alone costs more than we made in a month as teenagers, and the bag - Chanel - more than double our monthly salaries, and..."

"Enough!" Noah spins around and looks at Daisy angrily. "Shut up, Daisy. Why do you think Cara never told you who her parents were and where she got the money? Because she hates that kind of prejudice. Leave her alone."

I am more than surprised by his outburst and my heart starts beating faster when I realize that he defended me. Is that a step in the right direction?

"That her clothes cost so much is a fact!" Daisy looks at him challengingly. "And you said yourself she's a spoiled brat who gets everything handed to her on a silver platter."

Jamie spits out his beer and the others gasp. I stare at Noah with big eyes. Why does he talk about me like that? Especially in front of Daisy, who obviously thinks I'm pretty shitty.

"You said that about me?" I ask sadly, trying to pull myself together. "To her?" I nod and point at Daisy.

"No!" Noah shakes his head. "Yes... I don't know. Not exactly ... not in those words."

"In what words then?" I want to know.

"Do we have to settle this now?" he asks.

"I don't know," I answer. "At least you're talking to me again. But I don't know if I want to. I have to get out of here."

I jump up from my chair and reach for my purse. I pull out a ten-dollar bill and slam it down on the table. It's way too much for a drink, but I don't feel like waiting any longer.

"Cara," Emily says, trying to stop me, but I slap her hand away.

"I need my stuff," I say.

"What?" she asks.

"I need my things," I repeat. "I want to go home. Where everyone is as spoiled as I am."

Emily bites her lip, but finally stands. She seems uncomfortable with the whole thing, as does everyone else at the table - except Daisy. She grins at me smugly, as if she has finally achieved her goal.

"I didn't call you a spoiled brat," Noah says, standing up. "But showing up here, with my friends, after everything that's happened... don't you think it's a little presumptuous?"

"I talked her into it," Emily says, and Noah gives her a dirty look.

"Stay out of it," he tells her.

"Leave her alone," I defend my new friend, "What are you doing, Noah?"

"What, Cara?" he hisses, pointing at the people at the table. "These are my friends; this is my home and you come here and..."

"What am I supposed to do?" I yell, unable to believe we're discussing this right now. "You've been ignoring me for weeks, even canceling our professional appointments. I didn't see any other way out but to come here. I just want us to talk again and sort this out."

"It's all settled for me," he says. I throw my hands up in the air in disbelief and can't help but laugh. Is it all settled for Noah? Is he making it so easy for himself because he's offended?

"I'm leaving," I say, looking at Emily. "Are you coming or not?"

She looks around apologetically and follows me out of the bar. I just want to get out of here.

"Cara!" she calls after me as I step out of the bar, completely dazed. "I'm sorry."

"You?" I stop and turn around.

"Yes, of course," she replies, embarrassed. "I didn't know that he... and... and my sister. I really didn't. I only meant well because I want things to work out with you."

"I know that," I say, running my fingers through my hair, "but it's completely fucked and Daisy's and Noah's words and ... I don't know what else to do."

Emily comes over and takes me in her arms. I cuddle up to her and sob.

"He ignores me and doesn't give me a chance to explain or apologize. Alex says he's here, but only because I ran into him at a Starbucks. I've done things wrong in the past, yes. But Noah hasn't done everything right either."

"I know," Emily sighs. "I'll take you home for now, okay? Then you can always fly to Boston in the morning."

197

"Okay," I say quietly and look back at the bar, hoping desperately that Noah will come out and talk to me, but the door doesn't move.

"Come on," she says, pushing me in front of her. "Tomorrow is another day."

22

CARA

The night on Emily's couch was anything but restful. That was partly because I lay awake half the night thinking about my fight with Noah. I still can't believe he talked to Daisy about me. To her of all people. Noah knows I want nothing to do with her.

I made a mistake and I wouldn't be traveling to this goddamn small town in Tennessee if I didn't care about him. I want to be with him.

"Don't look like that!" I jump up and look at Emily. She's sitting in the chair in front of me with a steaming cup of coffee in her hand. "It gives you wrinkles. Coffee?"

I pull myself up and take the cup from her.

"Thanks," I mumble. "That wasn't necessary."

"No problem," she says with a grin. "You look like you could use it."

"Hm," I say, sipping at my coffee. "I have to book a flight home."

Emily bites her lip and sighs.

"What is it?" I ask.

"Nothing," she says and sighs again. "Okay, but... you... you can't just leave like that. Don't you want to fight for Noah?"

"Fight for Noah?" I hiss, almost spilling the hot coffee on

my hand. Emily takes it back and puts it on the coffee table. "He told Daisy I was a spoiled brat. Why would I fight for him?"

"Because you love him," Emily says, standing up. "And my sister likes to dramatize things."

"He admitted he said that."

"He said he didn't say it that way, and I believe him. He wouldn't say you're a spoiled brat. Never!" I roll my eyes and grab my coffee. "Cara!"

"What?" I hiss and Emily flinches. "I'm sorry... I ... I shouldn't take my bad mood out on you. How can you put up with that ... that person?"

"With Daisy?" Emily raises her eyebrows. Then she smiles. "For one thing, she's my sister, and one day she might be all I have. And for another, she's okay ... most of the time."

"She throws herself at two guys at once," I continue. "If Alex isn't available, she'll just spread her legs for Noah and..."

"She's still my sister!" Emily interrupts me harshly. "She can be a pain, yes. And what she did yesterday wasn't okay, but she's still my sister. Please don't talk about her like she's a slut. You don't know her, Cara."

"I'm sorry," I say, burying my face in my hands. "I ... I just don't know what to believe anymore. He can't... he didn't..."

"Noah with Daisy?" Emily asks and I nod. "No way. She can hit on him all she wants, he's nothing like Alex."

"Isn't he?" I ask hopefully and Emily laughs and goes into the kitchen. I get up from the couch and follow her. Her apartment is tiny and would be way too small for me.

"Tell me," I urge. "Isn't he?"

"No," Emily says, leaning against the counter. "He isn't. Alex never cheated on Daisy, but he would sometimes flirt. Noah, on the other hand, was never like that. For him, it was always about football."

"And yet you always liked Alex more than Noah."

It just slipped out, even though it's none of my business. Besides, Alex is her big sister's ex-boyfriend. Emily's face turns bright red and she turns away. She is busy putting things together on the small table when I interrupt her.

"Em?" I ask shyly. "I'm sorry."

She sighs and turns to me. Her gaze is blank and her lips are drawn into a thin line.

"Don't be sorry," she assures me, trying to smile. "He'll never notice me anyway."

"Never notice..." I shake my head. "Don't say that!"

"Cara," she says, "let it go, okay? I've known Alex for over a decade. He dated my sister and still goes to bed with her. He's not interested in me - not like that."

"But at the Fall Fair..."

"He likes Daisy!" she hisses at me and apologizes immediately. "I didn't mean it like that ... he ... forget it."

"No," I say, reaching for her hand. "If you and Alex ..."

"Alex doesn't like me and never will. I'm like a little sister to him and Noah and look at me..." She points at her figure and then at mine. "And look at you or Daisy. That's what the McCarter twins are like."

"Don't make yourself so small," I beg her, "you're so pretty and..."

The ringing of the doorbell interrupts our conversation. Emily spins on her heel and rushes to the door. It's probably more than convenient for her that we can cut our conversation short.

I lean against the counter and wait for her to return. As soon as she leaves for work, I'll have to book a flight and have Marina pick me up in Boston. I'm going to miss Emily when I'm back in my life. Maybe we'll manage to stay in touch, but it would be better for everyone if we cut it off. She's part of

Noah's friends, his life, and there's no place for me in it.

"It's for you," Emily says with a smile and steps aside. Noah appears next to her. My heart immediately starts beating faster. He looks tired, his hands in the pockets of his jeans.

"I'm going to work and hopefully you'll still be here when I get back. The Tennessee adventure isn't over yet."

I can't help but laugh as she comes over and gives me a kiss on the cheek.

"Don't screw it up again," she whispers, "neither of you."

With a knowing smile, she waves and leaves the apartment.

Noah and I are left alone and I look at him in anticipation. What is he doing here? Is he going to take me to the airport to make sure I'm really leaving Nashville or is he going to give me another piece of his mind?

"Hey," he says quietly. "Are you free?"

"I don't have any plans," I answer with a grin and he returns it. "Do you want to go for a walk?"

"Okay," I say hesitantly, knitting my eyebrows together. "And... and then?"

"Shall we talk?" he answers. "Even if I don't deserve it after last night, I'd like to talk to you again. About everything."

"Everything?" I ask, my eyes widening. My stomach tingles treacherously and I grin at him. "You mean about us?"

"Yes," he says. "And how it should continue."

"Okay," I agree, brushing back a strand of my hair. "Then ... then I'm going to get dressed."

"I'll wait for you here."

★★★

At first, Noah and I walk side by side in silence, lost in our thoughts. I hadn't expected this turn of events. After all, he made it very clear to me last night that I should disappear from his life. And then he suddenly shows up at Emily's door and wants to talk. It's really confusing. For my head and especially for my heart. I want to be with him, and I've fallen in love with him. Noah is the man I want to spend the rest of my life with.

"I didn't say that you were a spoiled brat," he finally breaks the silence. "I would never say that about you."

Noah puts his hands in his jacket pockets and looks over at me.

"I get along with Daisy, always have. But I don't want anything from her."

"Hm." I shake my head. It's hard to believe, especially after her performance yesterday. There's no doubt she'd take him in a heartbeat if Alex wasn't around.

"Huh?" Noah asks, raising his eyebrows. "Hm, you don't believe me that I don't want anything from Daisy, or hm, you don't believe me that I didn't say that to her?"

"I believe you said it ... well ... at least not in those words," I reply. "And as for the other thing... I don't know."

"I never had anything to do with Daisy and I never will," he says clearly. His voice gets louder towards the end. "She's Alex's ex-girlfriend. That's a no-go for me. Besides, I'm only interested in one woman."

A gentle smile plays around his lips, telling me that he can only mean me. Heat rises inside me and my heartbeat accelerates again.

"I know how it all must have affected you yesterday, but damn ... I felt totally ambushed. You have to admit, I didn't expect you to show up here."

"What was I supposed to do?" I ask and stop. "You've been ignoring me for weeks, even forbidding Alex to contact me. What are you doing, Noah?"

"I needed space," he justifies.

"For so many weeks?" I retort, and raise my eyebrows. "You

can't be serious."

"Yes," he insists. "I am serious."

I puff out my cheeks and shake my head.

"What happened at the awards show was ... a disaster, and I felt so insulted."

"You felt insulted?" I ask. "You announced that I was taken when I was never taken. How was I supposed to react?"

Noah takes a deep breath and within seconds there is nothing left of his gentle expression.

"All you had to do was admit that you felt more than friendship for me. That's all I asked, Cara. Of course, I didn't think it was funny that this Dick..."

"Brick," I correct him.

"Brick," he snarls. "Was hitting on you. I heard you say it. We were never just friends, Cara. At least from my end. I wanted to know you from day one."

"Noah, I..."

"No," he cuts me off harshly. "You listen to me now! I understand that you're scared and worried about your childhood and your father. And yes, I can't offer you a life like a mechanic or a lawyer can, but I ... I just want you. You've been the only woman in my life for weeks. When we first met... you... you walked into the room and... and I was completely taken by you. After Alex finally persuaded me to talk to you and I blew it the first time, you weren't there when I came back."

I look at him with a grin, because I remember our first meeting very well.

"I tried everything to convince you and after we had sex for the first time, you got to know my family and we spent more and more time together ..." He takes a deep breath. "I ... I thought it would be easy."

"Noah ... you can't believe that," I mumble. "We didn't just get together out of the blue. It didn't even come up that you wanted a serious relationship."

"But we're not teenagers anymore and we're always asking if we're together," he replies. "And to me, that's what we were - together."

"Noah, I..." I stammer. "I made a mistake, and yes, it shouldn't have escalated like that at the awards show, but I... I felt so trapped and I... I had my principles."

"Fuck your principles!" he yells. "Forget them, Cara. I'm here and I want to be with you. I want to make you happy and..."

"And you're a football player."

"That's right," he says. "But we both live in Boston and we might be apart two days every two weeks. Sometimes three weeks in the summer because I'm at training camp. And ... and if you don't want kids because ... because I don't have time, we'll wait. That's not a problem, but please, give us a chance."

I stare at him open-mouthed and can't make a sound.

Noah sighs and takes a step towards me. "Please?"

"Maybe I got a little carried away," I admit. "And maybe I should have done things differently."

"Maybe?" Noah raises his eyebrows and grins. "Don't you think you should take the 'maybe' out of that sentence?"

"Yeah, okay!" I call. "I'll cross it out. I should have given you a chance and not put my stupid principles before my happiness."

"It's okay," he says, taking a step toward me. "Seriously, Cara. I want this. I want you and no other woman. I'm not interested in another woman."

"Daisy?"

He groans in annoyance and rolls his eyes.

"I mean it this time," I insist. "What did you say to her? Where did you get the idea to tell her that?"

He runs his hands over his face and moans.

"I was frustrated and I got drunk with her..."

"With her?" I hiss. "Noah!"

"Nothing happened between us and nothing ever will. Daisy loves Alex."

I roll my eyes. The stupid cow should stay away from both McCarter twins. It would be best for everyone.

"I was drunk and I told her that you were acting like a brat and that everything had to be your way. And that's exactly what you did, Cara!"

"Pff!" I look at him in disbelief. "I can't believe you'd say that."

"Jesus Christ!" he shouts, grabbing my hand to pull me toward him. "I want you, only you. You're the only woman I want to be with, Cara Catherine Corse. And either you tell me right now that you want that too, or..." Noah stops dramatically and I open my eyes.

Why is he doing this?

My heart races, afraid that everything between us might be over again.

"Or?" I whisper.

"Or we go our separate ways forever," he answers. "I want you. Only you, but you have to want me as well. It won't work otherwise."

"I want you too," I say, putting my hand on his cheek. I stroke it gently and smile at him. "I want you and that's why I'm here. I shouldn't have done all this and ... and I should have allowed my feelings for you. It was easier for me to talk myself into the friendship thing than to really deal with where it was taking us. That was wrong, and enough people have told me that by now."

"Oh yeah?" he asks. "Who?"

"My mom, Alex, Emily..." I sigh. "You want me to list

others?"

I tug on his jacket and smile. Noah returns my smile and leans into me. Our eyes lock and despite his clothes, I can feel his heart beating hard beneath my fingers.

"I love you," he says.

"I love you too," I reply, sealing his mouth with mine.

Noah kisses me back and pulls me closer. His arms wrap around me and I wrap mine around his neck at the same time, pulling him closer.

EPILOGUE

NOAH

The sun's rays awaken me as they shine through the large panoramic windows. Everything in me resists opening my eyes for fear of waking up from the wonderful dream I've been in since yesterday afternoon. Cara plays the main role in it. We've reconciled and she's finally the woman at my side.

A discussion was more than necessary. I was almost sorry that I had ignored her for so long. After she broke my heart at the awards show, I needed some space. I couldn't just go back to normal and pretend the conversation never happened.

Now I'm sure everything's going to be fine. We're together and that's all that matters.

I love Cara and she loves me.

She is the woman of my dreams and I can't imagine spending my life without her.

With a gentle movement, I push Cara's body away from me. She mumbles something and I'm afraid I've woken her, but I haven't. My girlfriend turns over on her other side and continues to sleep blissfully. I run my eyes down her naked back and butt before getting out of bed and pulling on my boxers. Then I leave the bedroom and go downstairs to make us breakfast. Since I've been sleeping at my house instead of at my parents' for the last few days, the fridge is full. Alex and I usually use the house as a place to sleep so we don't get on our parents' nerves or have to keep an eye on our mother.

It sits on a large piece of land that we bought two years ago. Next to this house, which belongs to the previous owner, there are two unused lots. Alex and I plan to build our own houses there someday.

Since I arrived in Nashville, my mom has been pestering me with questions about Cara. The newspaper articles were everywhere, even in Tennessee. Trying to make her understand that Cara was over didn't work very well. Instead, she wanted to motivate me to talk to Cara and forgive her.

Today, the story is very different. Cara and I are together and we want to give each other a chance.

In a good mood, I grab a carton of eggs from the refrigerator and a frying pan from the bottom drawer to make scrambled eggs and bacon for breakfast. I put the pan on the ceramic stove top and drizzle some oil on it.

"Good Morning!" I jump at the sound of her voice and turn around.

"Did I wake you?" I ask and she shakes her head. Cara comes over with a smile and wraps her arms around me from behind. Her hands run down my stomach to my boxers, making it hard for me to concentrate. I definitely hadn't planned on her hands on my skin and her nimble fingers on the waistband of my shorts.

"No," she whispers, kissing my bare shoulder. "The bed was cold and empty."

I can't help but laugh.

"I'm making breakfast," I explain, pointing to the frying pan.

"What?" Cara glances past me and I give her a quick look.

"Scrambled eggs with bacon. Sorry, we don't have anything else."

"It's fine," she replies, "can I help you?"

"You can set the table and make the coffee."

She nods and turns away.

The silence behind me makes me skeptical, and it occurs to me that she doesn't even know where to find the utensils. How stupid of me.

"Sorry," I say, turning around. "You can't possibly know where the things are..."

My eyes almost pop out when I see her.

Cara is wearing her thin robe. We picked up her clothes from Emily's earlier. The robe is open and I stare at her. She's sitting naked on the kitchen table in front of me, grinning. "Maybe you're hungry for something else, too," she says, biting her lips.

I gasp for air and my dick in my boxer shorts instantly gets hard. "I am..." Luckily, my brain hasn't completely stopped thinking and I'm at least able to turn around and turn off the stove before I walk up to Cara, wrap my arms around her waist and kiss her. Cara kisses me back and wraps her arms around my neck. I pull her closer, pushing the robe off her shoulders and looking at her beautiful body.

My hard dick presses against her intimacy and she moans in pleasure as I rub against her.

"Noah!" She gasps and moans as I pull her thin panties down to her knees and explore her pussy with my fingers. I quietly explore her wet center and slide two fingers inside her. Cara's fingernails dig into my shoulders, and my lips seek hers again. The kiss is hot and uninhibited. We each want the upper hand as our tongues play around each other. I add a third finger to stretch it.

My lips leave hers and roam down her neck and décolleté. Her stiff nipples reach out to me. I take them between my lips and suck them. The little buds harden more and more.

211

Cara stretches her pelvis towards me and accepts my every thrust with pleasure. This woman is so infinitely hot that I still can't believe she's mine. I circle her clit with my thumb.

Cara is everything I've ever looked for and everything I want. She knows life as a football player like no other woman, and she knows exactly what to expect in the years to come. But after that, we still have all the time in the world to enjoy our life together. And when we have kids and start a family, we'll find ways to see each other as much as possible. I'm sure we will.

My lips reach her belly button, and she lies back on the table. Grinning, I pull my fingers out of her and look at them.

"Noah," she whispers, spreading her legs a little wider. "Please!"

"Please what?" I tease her, putting her thighs over my shoulders so that her wet sex is right in front of me. I lean forward gently and kiss her clit. Cara moans. Her pelvis rises, but I gently push her back down onto the tabletop.

I kiss the soft skin on the inside of her thighs and slowly work my way up to her pussy. Her moans get louder and louder and when I spread her labia with my fingers to get better access with my mouth, she cries out.

Cara's legs tighten around my neck and I fear she can't hold out much longer. She's almost ready even though I haven't really started yet.

"Hold on," I urge her, slipping my left hand into my boxers and cupping my cock. As expected, it's more than hard. "Just a few more minutes."

"I can't do it," she gasps and I let my tongue rub over her pulsating clit. "Noah, please ... I ... fuck ..."

Cara's entire body rears up. Her heels slam into my shoulders and I continue to lick her as her orgasm crashes over her.

"Oh my God!" she cries out in pleasure.

I straighten up and pull her off the table. She looks up at

me in amazement. Her cheeks are flushed and her own pleasure is running down the inside of her legs.

"You're so damn beautiful," I whisper to her as my fingers
play with her clit again. The sensitive bundle of nerves is completely overstimulated.

"I want you," she whispers.

Smiling, I help her to remove her robe and throw it and our
underwear on the floor. She is completely naked in front of me.
Her upper body is still rising and falling with effort. I look at
her for a moment. The milky skin, her small firm breasts that
fit perfectly in my hands, and the delightful nipples stretching
towards me.

"You feel so good," I whisper, wrapping my lips around her
right nipple. Cara gasps as I bite down on it and lick it with my
tongue. I give the left nipple the same attention while rolling
the right one between my thumb and forefinger.

"Noah, please," Cara whispers, her pelvis bucking. "Take
me."

"With pleasure," I reply, wrapping her legs around my hips.
Without taking my eyes off her, I position my glans between
her labia. Centimeter by centimeter I penetrate Cara. Her
tightness welcomes me and, as always, it feels phenomenal to
be inside her. I push against her as far as I can. She gasps and
I press my lips together not to come too soon.

Then I push into her at a leisurely pace.

★★★

"It's so nice here!" exclaims Cara.

Wearing a warm winter jacket, which is way overkill for today's temperatures, and a hat with the Nashville Warriors logo
on it, Cara is way overdressed, but she doesn't care. Hand in
hand we stroll through Old Nashville and enjoy the quiet life

in Tennessee before we fly back to Boston tonight.

I really appreciate this time with my girlfriend, I still can't believe it!

"And then you're moving to Boston?" she asks, looking up at me.

"Well," I say, pulling her closer. "I can't complain about my time in Boston so far."

"That's true." She grins. "Let's go in here."

She points to a cupcake shop.

"Sure," I say, following her. In fact, I would follow her into any store and buy her anything she wants. As long as it makes her happy and keeps us together. Fortunately, no one can read my mind, because I sound like a fool in love.

Love really does make you blind and certainly a little stupid, but I can't complain.

The little bell above the shop door rings as we push open the door and enter.

"Wow!" Cara says, rushing to the display. All kinds of cupcakes are stacked up there. I read through the flavors and am quite surprised at what's available. How the hell is Jack Daniel's whiskey supposed to taste in a cupcake?

"Hello," a young woman about our age says, smiling at us. Until she recognizes me, then her eyes literally pop out of her head. "Oh God... you... you're... Noah McCarter."

I look at Cara and she grins.

"I am," I confirm with a smile and shove my hands into my pockets. "My girlfriend likes your cupcakes."

Her eyes dart to Cara and then back to me until she grabs a pair of disposable gloves.

"Would you like to try some, miss?" she asks nicely.

Cara is clearly uncomfortable that the young woman is treating us so kindly and would surely let us try any cupcake we wanted. But that's life as a football star - especially in your hometown.

"Maybe one or two, but we don't want to cause any trouble," my friend coyly dismisses.

"You're not trouble," she replies, pointing to a high table in the corner. "I'll bring you a selection of our bestsellers. Do you have any allergies?"

I shake my head and Cara does the same.

"Great!" Smiling, I grab Cara's hand and pull her with me away from the display to the table.

"I'm uncomfortable with this," she whispers. "I don't like being the center of attention."

"Baby," I reassure her, kissing her temple. "You said you wanted cupcakes."

"Yes," she says, "I did, but she's giving them to us for free and I don't want that. All her heart and soul, and certainly her money, goes into this place, and we..."

"I have an idea," I interject. "If we want to pay her and she refuses, let's offer her a deal."

"Like what?" Cara asks and I smile.

"Next week is a big game for our high school team. It's for the Tennessee high school championship finals. I'll get her a table there and she can sell her cupcakes."

"That's a great idea!" Cara exclaims and kisses me. "You're the best."

"I know," I reply cockily as the young owner sets two plates and a bottle of water in front of us. It's way too much. I certainly couldn't forgive myself for not giving her something in return.

"These are the current bestsellers," she says. "A raspberry with Oreo cookies and Kinder chocolate. A friend of mine was an au pair in Germany and brought some of this chocolate back. Try it."

"Before we do," Cara says. "I'm Cara and this is Noah. And

you are?"

"I'm Hannah," she says, "Nice to meet you. Try it."

I grab one of those kids' chocolate cupcakes and take a bite. Cara takes the raspberry one.

"Would you... like to try the one with Jack Daniel's whiskey?"

"Sure," I say and she disappears again. I turn to Cara and grin at her. "And?"

"Wow," she says, "you have to try this one." She holds her cupcake in front of me, and I take a bite.

"Eww," I say, tightening my mouth. "Too sweet."

"Nonsense," she keeps eating with delight. "And yours?"

"They're really great," I reply. "They have some really interesting chocolate in Germany."

"Do you like it?" Hannah asks excitedly. "Here's the one with Jack Daniels."

She puts it down and smiles at me.

"How long have you had the shop?" I ask.

"Just three months," she explains, "I trained as a pastry chef and this was my big dream."

"That sounds expensive," Cara speculates and Hannah nods.

"It is," she says, "the rent for the shop, the loan I had to take out for the kitchen appliances, and finally the weekly groceries. But I'm not complaining. It's my big dream."

"That means you need advertising, right?" I ask, taking a bite of the Jack Daniels muffin. Hannah nods and takes a cupcake as well.

"Advertising is always good," she replies, "to make me better known."

"The Tennessee High School Championship semifinals are in two weeks," I explain. "I could get you a booth there."

Hannah's eyes light up, and she looks at Cara. She smiles

at her.

"Really?" she asks, "That... that's not necessary."

"About four thousand people are coming to the game," I continue to bribe her. "If only half of them buy a cupcake..."

"Oh my God!" she squeals. "But... that... I can't pay in advance. It'll be too expensive."

"I'll take care of it," Cara says, and Hannah looks at her in surprise. "Send me a list of all the ingredients and everything you need. I'll pay for it."

"But ... but I can't accept that."

"Yes, you can," my friend continues unperturbed. "I'm happy to do it."

Hannah still looks surprised and doesn't know what to say to Cara's offer.

"Come on," Cara urges.

"Okay," Hannah agrees. "Thank you very much."

"Perfect! Do you have a piece of paper and a pen? I'll write down my contact information for you." Cara looks around searchingly.

Hannah nods and goes to the cash register.

★★★

After Cara and I leave the cupcake shop, we walk in silence behind each other. Something seems to be bothering her. I squeeze her hand, forcing her to look at me.

"What's wrong with you?" I ask. "You're so pensive."

"Yes," she says, "I am. Hannah has put all her money into this place and must have so much debt because of it."

"That's the way it is when you..."

"Don't say it," she replies, "really, Noah. I was wondering if we could do something about it." I stop and look at her.

"What do you mean?" I ask.

"I was thinking about a foundation," she explains. "Young people like Hannah can send us their business plan, and if we like it, then ... we fund it. That way they don't start their own business with a pile of debt."

I look at my friend for a moment and am completely taken aback by this suggestion. I wasn't expecting it at all, but I think it's a good idea. It's a great idea and neither Cara nor I lack the financial means.

"You think it's stupid, don't you?" she asks when I don't react immediately.

"No," I say hastily. "I don't think so. I think it's good. With our high profile, we would certainly find a lot of investors."

"Especially my dad," she continues. "And we could really do some good with our money."

"Yes," I say, smiling at her. "We should talk to your dad when we get home."

"Really?" she asks, pausing. "Are you serious?"

"Baby," I sigh and put my hand on her cheek. "I'm going to support you with your idea. I'll even be a brand ambassador for the whole thing. And my brothers too. I absolutely agree with you that it's unacceptable that young people have to be heavily in debt before they can build their own lives."

Cara screams and jumps into my arms. I take a step back and put my hands on her butt.

"You're the best," she whispers, putting her mouth on mine. "I guess some principles are meant to be broken."

"I thought they were resolutions?"

"Principles, resolutions," she says, "all unnecessary when you're much happier without them, and you make me happy, Noah McCarter."

"You make me happy too," I say, kissing her again. "Cara Catherine Corse."

"I love you."

"I love you too," I reply.

ABOUT THE AUTHOR

How could it be otherwise, sport - ball sports to be precise - got Mrs Kristal into writing. She wrote her first stories in 2012, and her first attempts at writing about football developed over the years into real stories and eventually books.

Thematically, Mrs. Kristal switched continents and wrote about American football from then on. In 2021, she published her first book about college romance and football. Mrs. Kristal draws inspiration from everyday situations, memories of experiences and conversations with friends and family.

In addition to sport, her books always focus on love and friendship. What she particularly loves about writing is that she can immerse herself in other worlds, accompany her characters on a long journey and there is a happy ending at the end. When Mrs. Kristal is not writing, she spends time with her friends and family and travels the world. One of her greatest wishes - to have seen the countries, cities and stadiums she writes about once in her life.

By the same author:
Lincoln Tigers Series (College Football Romance)
> *Perfect Roommate*
> *Perfect Playboy*
> *Perfect Baby Daddy*
> *Perfect Forever*

Our books are also available in e-book. Find our catalog on:
https://cherry-publishing.com/en/

Subscribe to our newsletter and receive a free e-book! You'll also receive the latest updates on all of our upcoming publications!

https://mailchi.mp/b78947827e5e/get-your-free-ebook

Editorial manager: Audrey Puech
Composition and layout: Cherry Publishing
Interior Illustrations: © Shutterstock
Cover design: Keti Matakov
Cover illustration: Keti Matakov

Printed in Great Britain
by Amazon

43682308R00128